W9-CAO-750

BROWSING COLLECTION
14-DAY CHECKOUT
No Holds • No Renewals

THE
CHRISTMAS
GUEST

ALSO BY PETER SWANSON

WILLIAM MORROW

An Imprint of HarperCollins*Publishers*

THE CHRISTMAS GUEST

GUEST

A NOVELLA

PETER SWANSON

THE CHRISTMAS GUEST. Copyright © 2023 by Peter Swanson. All rights reserved. Printed in the United States of America. No part of this book may be used or reproduced in any manner whatsoever without written permission except in the case of brief quotations embodied in critical articles and reviews. For information, address HarperCollins Publishers, 195 Broadway, New York, NY 10007.

HarperCollins books may be purchased for educational, business, or sales promotional use. For information, please email the Special Markets Department at SPsales@harpercollins.com.

FIRST EDITION

Designed by Kyle O'Brien

Title page art © MaxNadya/Shutterstock

Library of Congress Cataloging-in-Publication Data has been applied for.

ISBN 978-0-06-329745-6

23 24 25 26 27 LBC 5 4 3 2 1

For two aunts—
Pearl Taylor Moynihan,
who disliked Christmas,
and for Sue Ellis Swasey,
who doesn't particularly like it either

"I wear the chain I forged in life," replied the Ghost.

—Charles Dickens, *A Christmas Carol*

THE
CHRISTMAS
GUEST

ONE

Since I have no family of my own, I am yearly asked by friends and colleagues to their homes for the Christmas holidays. I always say no, pleading my case that I am perfectly content to be alone for a week. And mostly I am. I read a good book, maybe rewatch some of my favorite films. On Christmas Day, I roast a chicken and eat it with crispy potatoes and Brussels sprouts. My cat, Elspeth, likes a bit of roast chicken too, and I let her sit on the kitchen counter as a special treat. In the afternoon I often clean my apartment or reorganize my bookshelves. Sometimes, if the weather is nice, I'll take a walk across Manhattan, see if there is a movie playing that looks interesting.

I am not completely alone. The doorman Howard and I usually find time for a glass of whiskey, and I have a close friend, also without family, who often drops by, although she hasn't for the past couple of years.

This year, Christmas Day has arrived on the heels of a wet, sleety nor'easter that rattles the windows of my apartment, so after my roast chicken I decide to skip the walk and tackle my bedroom closet. I am lucky enough to live in a two-bedroom apartment, and I'm slightly embarrassed to say that I've turned the second bedroom into a walk-in closet. But I work in fundraising, and sometimes I feel as though half my life is spent at galas and cocktail parties. I need a lot of dresses and a lot of shoes.

The closet in my bedroom has become my default storage space, filled with boxes containing mementos of my past lives, all that bric-a-brac that is impossible to throw away, and yet completely useless. I open the door gingerly, expecting an avalanche of photo albums and souvenirs to tumble out. That would make for quite a New York story: lonely single woman crushed to death while cleaning closet on Christmas Day—cat kept alive by remaining roast chicken dinner. But the boxes stay aloft long enough for me to remove them from the closet one by one and place them on the floor. My goal is to throw away maybe a quarter of what I've kept. I start with a box that I must have filled during my first few years in New York City. I find a packet of photographs that chronicle a New Year's Eve party in the East Village (worth keeping) and a DVD box set of *Seinfeld* seasons one and two that goes directly in the trash. I tell myself this is going to be easier than I thought.

By the time I've turned on the lamps in my apartment, I've been through almost all the boxes and filled two small trash bags. I'm working on the oldest boxes now, including one that smells like mothballs and contains my grandmother's purse and another that has a childhood doll I'm loath, for some reason, to throw out. Underneath my birth certificate and my canceled passports, I find an immediately recognizable diary, white Moleskine with a ribbon bookmark, and pick it up, scooching backward along the Persian rug to rest against my bed. I flip through the pages, arriving at an entry from December 1989. Exactly thirty years ago. I decide to take a look, not entirely sure that I'm prepared to go back in time to that annus horribilis, that murderous year, but also knowing that once I start to read I won't be able to stop.

There is a famous quote, the first line from L. P. Hartley's *The Go-Between*, a book about remembering (although every book is a book about remembering, isn't it?). "The past is a foreign country: they do things differently there." In my case the past really is a foreign country. And, yes, they do things very differently there.

December 17

Emma Chapman, the one who looks like me, has invited me to her house for Christmas! I tried to be cool and pause for five seconds pretending to consider my options but I don't think I fooled her. So I just went ahead and accepted, and she looked pleased. She told me that it would be her parents, who were Satan's spawn; her twin brother, who was basically nice; plus a host of friends and endless cousins. Not too many, she said.

I know I've mentioned Emma to you, Dear Diary. Met her during orientation week. Wears cashmere and jewelry that looks like stuff I'll never in my lifetime be able to afford. Sounds posh, or at least that's what other students say. Every time we talk I say something stupid that I end up repeating in my head again and again, and then there was that time when she told me that she liked Stuart Montgomery and I forgot about it and hooked up with him and felt awful. In other words, I just assumed she hated my guts. I mean she was always friendly but I thought she was just being English. But now that she's invited me to her house for Christmas, who knows? Am I her best friend? Ha ha.

I asked her how big her house was and she said, Don't worry, I'd have my own room.

I had so many questions but she'd invited me between classes and there wasn't time to ask them. She said she was chuffed I could come, and that she'd be at the pub in the union tomorrow night and if I met her there she'd give me all the details.

I'm EXCITED (chuffed, I guess is the correct word), and even though I'd prepared myself to be alone in London over Christmas, part of me even looking forward to it, I am now so happy that I'm going to be with people. Nervous, too, though. What will the family be like? Are my clothes nice enough? Will they expect me to go grouse hunting? Do I need to bring presents? I guess I'll find out everything tomorrow.

December 18

Today was not a good day. I pretty much know that I flunked my British Landscapes exam. My brain was frozen all during it, and afterward I double-checked the textbook and I'd misidentified a Turner painting as a Constable. So there was that. I went back to my flat in the afternoon and Jody had left all her breakfast dishes on the table. I considered moving them to her bedroom but decided against it. She's gone in two days and I'll never see her again so what difference does it really make? Still, it put me in a foul mood.

Then I went to the pub, expecting to see Emma, and I figured if anything could cheer me up it would be that. I couldn't wait to hear more about our Christmas holidays. But I sat at a table by myself for an hour and she didn't show. I was about to leave when Tom, that kid from Florida who always wears a baseball cap, showed up and I had a few drinks with him, told him how I wasn't going back to America for the Christmas break and he just kept asking me why, and finally, probably because I'd had about six ciders, I told him that my mom was dead and I didn't know who my father was, so I was basically an orphan. I hadn't wanted to tell him because I thought he'd be full of pity and I wasn't in the mood for it, but it turned out he was pretty rude about my orphan status, saying something like, You must have friends, though, right? I told him I had friends, thinking of Michelle, so in love now with her college boyfriend that I barely heard from her (WAAH!).

I did let him walk me back to my flat, and he reminded me about that party back in September when we'd fooled around, and I said that I'd grown up a lot since then. Ha ha, he said and tried to kiss me anyway, but honestly, I wasn't in the mood. I had a pretty decent memory of the time we'd fooled around and it hadn't exactly been pleasant (neck licker, for one, and his shirt smelled). I went up to my flat, where I could hear Jody fucking that professor from her program, and I clopped as loudly as I could into the kitchen, ate a bowl of leftover mashed potatoes, and, while I didn't wash the dishes she'd left on the table, I gritted my teeth and put them into the sink to soak in warm water. Then I got into bed and wrote to you, Dearest Diary.

December 19

It's morning and I'm still under the covers. All I have to do to-day is turn in the essay I've already written on art in Weimar Germany and then meet with my adviser, Nicola. It's occurred to me that I could try to find Emma—I'm pretty sure that she'll be taking her last exam today in Somerset House and I could skulk around outside and hope to run in to her. But maybe she's decided she doesn't want me to come home with her for Christmas after all, and if that's the case then it'll just be embarrassing for both of us. I was resigned to being alone in London already, so I'll just have to become resigned again. I'll go to all the museums I haven't gone to yet. I'll do the student standby thing and go to the theater. And if it's not too cold I'll try to start running again. Michelle told me I would gain about twenty pounds when I lived in London and honestly she wasn't that far from the truth. Less cider, no more potatoes, more running! Go back to the Leighton House and pay attention this time. Eat at that Indian place with the blue walls again.

And, who knows, maybe get a head start on my coursework for next semester. That would be amazing. The more I think about it, the more I think it's best that I'm alone over Christmas. It'll be good for me.

Well, I'm back, and I'm just a little bit drunk, and I've spent all night with Emma, and not only am I going to her family's house in the Catswolds!!! but I'm going tomorrow!

After I met with Nicola and she assured me that I had defi-nitely not flunked British Landscapes, I went straight to the Dragon, which was packed of course because it was last day of term. *Debbie and Tom and that other American girl whose name I can never remember were all there and I had drinks with them, and then I saw Emma up at the bar and I didn't know what to do, but she turned and saw me and ran over to tell me how sorry she was that she didn't make it the night before and how she realized she didn't have my number or anything.*

Short story long she told me that it was all settled for me to come to her house but that she couldn't give me a ride. She was totally embarrassed I think but her brother was driving her home tonight—he lives in London too—and she would have invited me to go with them but my room wasn't ready yet and "Mummy" had said no visitors till Wednesday, and etcetera, etcetera, and would I mind taking the train tomorrow afternoon and she'd pick me up at the station. I told her that I'd love to take the train and she hugged me and got my number at the flat and told me she'd call me in the morning with the train time and all that. I kept asking her questions about what I should wear and what I should bring, and she kept laughing and told me to wear whatever I want and don't bring anything, which wasn't helpful. Then she put her hand on my cheek and stared into my eyes and told me how excited she was that I'd be there for Christmas and I realized she was pretty drunk too.

Hopefully she'll actually call tomorrow.

December 20

I'm on the train to Clevemoor! It hasn't moved yet so I'm still at Paddington Station but I can't believe I'm actually going to an English country house for Christmas! It sounds like the beginning of a romance novel, or else maybe a murder mystery. Either one is far better than staying in London and getting lonely and depressed.

Emma called me in the morning. She said she was calling from Starvewood Hall, and I said, Your house has a name! and she laughed and told me that most houses in the country had a name and not to be too impressed. She had looked up train times and told me that I could catch a 1:35 from Paddington that would go direct. She said that she'd either pick me up herself or she'd send her brother. I asked her again what to bring and she said nothing. Still, this morning, I went on a manic shopping spree, buying two new pairs of tights, a white cable-knit sweater, a new headband that doesn't smell as though I haven't taken it off for two months, and some new underwear because you never know. Then I went to the Body Shop and bought foot creams and lotions to give to Emma and maybe her mum, then I panicked about the brother and her father and wound up going to a liquor store and spending practically all the money I have in the world on a bottle of scotch that the man in the shop told me was gift-worthy, and on a bottle of port that had a pretty label.

My bag weighs a ton but I'm on the train and it has actually started moving. Except for the Tube I haven't been on a train while living here and I thought I might be in one of those cabins you see in the movie with a glass door, everyone smoking. But I'm on an upholstered two-seater facing the wrong way, and the man next to me smells like onion soup. The fabric on the seats is the crazy pattern of blues and golds. The oniony man has fallen asleep, his shoulder pressed up against mine.

The train has cleared London and while there's no actual blue *showing in the sky it isn't raining or snowing, and five minutes ago I saw a flock of sheep on the side of a hill. I can't quite believe this is my life. A year ago I was in California, probably about to take the bus to my cousin's house in Carbondale, feeling sorry for myself, feeling like my life was never going to change. But it did change, and I'm on this train, and Emma said I should stay a whole week at least, that there was the dearest country pub walking distance from the house and that at least one of her cousins was semi-cute. I asked her what everyone did during the week, and she told me that what she did all day was read books or take country walks. She said it rather more charmingly, something like, Oh, be lazy, get fat, walk to the end of the garden and back, start drinking at lunch.*

I can feel my mind beginning to race with fantasies about what might happen this week. Slow down, mind! Just let it happen. Maybe it will be horrible and awkward and Emma will turn out to be the cold snob that I first thought she was when we met back in September. If that's the case, then at least I'll have a story to tell. That's what my mom always used to say.

Quick list, not that I'll follow any of it:

1. *Don't keep telling English people how quaint they are.*
2. *When in doubt, ask the person you're talking to what they've read recently, and if they've seen any good films.*
3. *Check teeth after lunch for embedded foodstuff.*
4. *It is not your job to fill any silence that lasts more than three seconds.*
5. *Wine is a sipping beverage.*
6. *Finish a book. Any book.*

A quick jot to say that I'm at the house. How do I describe it? It's a huge stone manor down a long gravel driveway. It's both kind of amazing and kind of run-down at the same time. There are endless rooms and the ceilings have beams across them and there are actual stained-glass windows in the parlor, which is what I would call the living room. The furniture is a little ragtag and all the rugs are so bare that in some places there's only half a rug left. My room is to the back of the house just at the top of a dark, narrow stairwell that leads up from the kitchen.

Servants' quarters? I said to Emma, who was giving me the tour and thank god she laughed, then she said, Yes, actually, although we haven't been able to afford a servant for five years. I laughed at that, thinking she was making a joke, but I don't think she was.

My room is cold as Canada but the window looks over the back garden, all rose bushes, some holding on to withered white flowers, all leading down to a little stone hut on the edge of a murky pond. Emma told me that there'd be drinks at six-ish in the parlor but that I could emerge before then and wander around. I'm happy, though, to sit at the little child's desk that's in this room and write to you, Dearest, until it's time to go down and meet the family. I do think (no, I know!) that I've been braver here in England than I've ever been in my life but I'm not brave enough to wander around introducing myself to random family members in a country house.

It is time to talk about Adam, the brother. When I got off the train at the tiny station (pale stone, like everything around here), he was waiting for me through the archway that led to the parking lot. He was leaning against his sporty car wearing a long tweedy coat over a threadbare polo shirt and smoking a cigarette. I spotted him first because he was staring at the back of his hand and this really is like the beginning of some gothic romance (or mystery movie!) because he's beautiful. Emma is beautiful too but in a way that isn't surprising. Honey hair, rosy cheeks, probably looks good naked. Her brother has the honey hair and the rosy cheeks as well but this kind of incredible roman nose and very wide shoulders so that his body narrows all the way down. And I realized that he's standing in contrapposto pose, one hip cocked, one knee bent, just like Michelangelo's David. He flicked his cigarette away and looked up and saw me, opening the trunk of his car for my bag but not offering to put it in for me. He did however offer me a cigarette and I said yes even though I'm only really a party smoker, but he was so aloof that I wanted to impress him. In the car I thanked him about a hundred times for picking me up so that eventually he had to tell me to stop thanking him. I stopped talking and figured that I'd already destroyed our love affair before it ever started. But then he said, Mind if we swing by this pub I know for a quick drink before heading back? I'm desperate.

I told him I didn't mind and he whipped the car in to a lane that I assumed was one way but cars kept coming from the other direction and I thought I was going to die about three times. I started saying BE COOL to myself, alternating it with NO MORE THANK-YOUS and we made it to the destination, me acting like I was squired by handsome boys to country pubs all the time, and that it was NO BIG DEAL.

Inside he asked me what I wanted and I forced myself to not say either Whatever's easiest or Whatever you're having and asked for a cider instead. I was glad I didn't ask for what he was *having because he got a double whiskey without ice. My cider was particularly good and we sat at a corner table by a fire that smelled like burning tar. The ceiling was incredibly low and there was a shaggy dog asleep by the fireplace and I had just assumed that all pubs in England were like pubs in London, but this was different. I felt as though I've gone back in time, the way I felt that first week in London when all the new students were taken on that architectural walk and we wound up at the Old Bell, a pub that Wren had designed, and if you squinted your eyes it was like you were there three hundred years ago.*

Cheers for this, Adam said, and explained how all his friends from town were at the Sheepfold, which was the pub near the house, and how he couldn't bear to see them but was gagging for a drink. I must have shivered because he pointed out that I didn't have a scarf (pressing the tip of his finger against my breastbone!) and offered me his, which I refused and buttoned up my jacket. I asked him about LSE—Emma told me he was going there, studying how to get rich—and he shrugged it off. I have a bad habit of filling pauses with inane conversation and I was trying hard not to speak, but wound up rambling about how pretty the pub was with its Christmas decorations. You like that sort of thing, do you? he said. I said, As much as the next girl, and that made him laugh. After he'd finished his drink he told me to drink up and then he drove me to the house, pointing out stuff along the way. Village green. House where some pop singer I hadn't heard of lived. The Sheepfold. And then we were suddenly at Starvewood Hall. Scene of the crime, he said, and he actually did carry my bag under the low threshold of the wide front door, dropping it onto the stone floor in the foyer. He shouted Emma's name until she showed up, looking annoyed and red-faced, and then left me with her.

A little drunk now, to be honest with you. Night was magical and now I need to get under the covers because I'm SO tired and SO cold. Met the parents and they are SCARY. More later. Emma stuck by my side all night. So sweet!! Dinner was buffet and we all ate in the dining hall and Adam was there but then he left for the pub. E and I were going to go too but then we curled up in front of the fire with a bottle of Baileys Irish Cream (best thing ever) and then I guess the pub was closed, and now I'm here, back in my cold room tucked up under a nubby blanket. The window is rattling and I keep hearing strange noises outside. Adam is beautiful. This might actually be a romance story (fingers crossed) but don't know how E would feel about it.

Do I care? Right now I don't suppose I do, but I always feel different in the morning. More later on this developing story.

December 21

Head throbbing, mouth like sandpaper. Ugh! Dreamt I was fooling around with Dave from back in high school and he was trying to find my breasts but they weren't there. Then woke up face-to-face with an orange cat, purring maniacally, and kneading away at my chest with its sharp claws. I sat up alarmed and the cat leapt off and went through my door (did I not shut it??) and now I'm awake and it's not even six but there's no way I'm falling back asleep.

Just read what I wrote yesterday and now I keep going over everything I said and did last night trying to figure out if I embarrassed myself or not. But it's all good. Emma is being so nice and I think I could tell her anything. She introduced me around but never left my side. Her mother was very cold and asked me where I was from in America and I said Sacramento in California, and she said, Yes, dear, I know where Sacramento is. Then later I called her Mrs. Chapman and she looked at me like I'd just spoken in a foreign language or something. Anyway, she goes on my list of people to avoid.

Mr. Chapman wasn't particularly friendly either but he did talk to me a little bit, asking me what job I hoped to get after my course in art history. I stammered on forever about how I was hoping to one day teach college and how it wasn't about a job for me but just my love of art and even thinking now of some of the things I said I'm cringing. We were both saved when his brother arrived with his wife and his four kids, two boys and two girls. Before Mr. Chapman went to greet them he briefly put his hand on the small of my back, sort of pushing me away, the way you'd push a plate away after eating all your food. I met the arriving family five minutes later in the parlor, the girls sullen teenagers, both pouty and skinny. Then there was a boy very tall and skinny as well with terrible acne who broke my heart a little. He must have been about fifteen. The older boy, Jeremy, taking some sort of gap year, was the one who E told me was kind of cute. He wore a rugby shirt and had a square jaw and I'm sure some girls would like him but I keep thinking about Adam, not that he has any interest in me whatsoever. Still, a girl can dream.

Dinner was some kind of pie filled with some kind of meat and even though I'm now calling myself a vegetarian I think it's smart to give all that up over the next week. It was so cozy in the parlor with the fireplace going and a large decorated tree. There are pine boughs everywhere, draped across the mantelpiece and around the doorways. I did feel as though I'd stepped into an enchanted fairytale life, so different from my own. I hope I'm describing this properly, Dear Diary, because one day, years from now, I might not remember and I want to create a picture for when I'm old. I love being here. And I love that I've been invited into a big messy family, full of cousins and friends. I loved that it was just Mom and me against the world when I was growing up, but my secret dream was being part of a large family. I tried to explain this to Emma and ended up telling her my whole sad life, how I never knew my father (WAAH!) and then my mother died of cancer, and she looked at me with hungry eyes and said, I know I shouldn't say this but that sounds amazing.

We all want what we don't have, I guess. (Profound thought for the day!)

And I want this, people coming and going—the neighbors, an older couple dressed as though they were in a Merchant Ivory film, swinging by last night for a quick drink. A friend of Adam's showing up and dragging him to the pub (away from me, BOO). Like I said last night Emma and I were going to go there as well, but we got far too cozy by the fire. I was disappointed, only because I wanted to spend time with Adam, but I loved being inside with E as well. One of the smelly dogs came and fell asleep on my feet.

Afternoon now. It's been a strange day. When I went down for breakfast it turned out that Emma was out walking with

Adam and I ended up eating with E's uncle Simon and his kids. The uncle barely spoke, and he made wincing sounds every time he took a bite of his toast. The girls—their names are Phoebe and Maggie, and I don't know which one is which—asked me questions about California. I told them I surfed (a little bit true) and that everyone has a cool car, but didn't tell them that Sacramento was the most boring city in America, or that most Californians are BORING. And I didn't tell them how lonely California can be compared to a village in England, that you have to drive to get to anywhere and that all my friends just cared about their clothes. Both the girls tried to imitate an American accent and sounded like they were from Texas. I did an English accent for them and they laughed and laughed and said it was terrible.

After breakfast I wandered a little through the house, feeling unmoored. I found E's mum and asked her if there was something I could do to help and she looked at me confused, as though I'd just asked her where I could buy drugs. Then she said, Of course not, dear, in a way that chilled my bones. I decided to take a walk, bundling up and putting on my Doc Martens, and asking Uncle Simon if he knew what direction Emma and Adam might have gone. He spent about ten minutes telling me that he didn't really know enough about the nearby walking paths, but then he said how he thought there was one that went around the pond, and how there was definitely some sort of path through the woods that brought you out to the other side of the village, etcetera, etcetera. I kept thanking him and taking a step toward the front door and then he'd tell me about another footpath he knew about. I don't miss a lot about home but I do miss the fact that when you ask someone in America for directions they don't try to help you if they don't know the way!

By the time I finally left the house, Adam and Emma were coming down the driveway. Emma apologized like mad that she hadn't waited for me to get out of bed before going on her walk and then she promised me that the two of us would go on a ramble later, and said that I should turn around and come back into the house with them. I was already cold from being outside during that conversation so it was an easy decision to stay with her and Adam.

For lunch Emma and Adam and I went to the Sheepfold. Jeremy, the older cousin, was already there when we arrived, holding a table for all of us, although Adam instantly spotted friends and went and sat with them. The pub was fancier than I thought it would be, with a whole dining area off to one side, lots of well-dressed older couples. The bar side was all dark wood and paintings of sheep and old shears on the walls. It felt as though Emma knew everyone who was there. A girl our age showed up, shrieked, and hugged her, and the two of them started talking rapidly, their heads practically touching. I was a little jealous. Jeremy was telling me about being on an archaeological dig on the island of Mallorca and I could tell that he was already a little drunk, and his spittle kept hitting my face whenever he got excited.

Groups of older people kept coming into the bar, having one drink, then being led into the dining room. Almost all of them either said hello or acknowledged Emma and Adam, but then one couple came in and it got a little strange. While the man was getting drinks at the bar, the woman—all done up in a Laura

Ashley dress and heavy makeup—kept staring at me, her eyes blinking rapidly. Then she was tugging at her husband's arm and pointing at me. E noticed and started looking around the room in a panicked sort of way, maybe looking for Adam, but then another older couple saw what was happening and went and intervened, the woman putting an arm around the one with the flowery dress. It was all very odd, and then I saw that Emma had caught Adam's eye from across the room, and I thought he'd come over, but instead he went the other way, through a low door that led to another section of the bar area, like he was running away.

I looked at E and said, What the fuck? Mouthing it more than saying it. She reached out a hand and said something I couldn't understand because of the loudness of the pub and then the new girl suddenly said very loudly, Oh my God, she does look just like her, and E shushed her.

Anyway, I got the whole story. The couple went to the dining room and then Adam came to our table, bringing us all another round. Apparently, back at the end of the summer a local girl from Clevemoor, still in high school, or secondary school, whatever you call it, had gone missing and then had been found dead in the nearby woods, murdered. Her name was Joanna Davies and that was her mother who was staring at me because I guess I look like her, like the murdered girl. You don't really, E said. Not your face, but I guess your size and your hair color and the way you wear it. No, she looks like her, Adam said. I had lots of questions but everyone said that it was a total mystery, that no one knew who had killed her, that the police were stumped.

When we left the pub, E was talking with her friend, so

Adam and I walked together about five feet behind them. We were each smoking one of his cigarettes and chatting away.

Me: *That was strange, wasn't it, what happened in the pub?*
Him: *I guess so.*
Me: *Did you know her, the girl?*
Him: *I did, actually. Emma didn't want to say anything because there are people around here who think I had something to do with it and it makes her crazy.*
Me: *Why do they think that?*
Him: *No good reason. It's just that we were friends. The police questioned me because I'd seen her shortly before she went missing, and now there's all sorts of rumors going around.*
Me: *Was she your girlfriend?*
Him: *(laughing a little) Define girlfriend.*
Me: *I'm not sure you need me to define that word. How about: Had the two of you kissed?*
Him: *Yes, we had. Is that what a girlfriend is?*

He said it very snarkily, and laughed. I was enjoying the conversation but aware that we were making jokes about a girl who had been murdered.

Me: *Well, do you kiss all your friends?*
Him: *Obviously. If they'll let me.*

Me: *Right. So she was just one of your friends that you also happened to kiss?*

Him: *Yeah, that sounds about right.*

I wanted to hear more but Adam bent and picked up a fallen apple and whipped it at his sister, hitting her in the back, and then she and her friend were off running, Adam chasing them.

I told E I was going to go read and take a nap but I really wanted to write to you, my Dearest D. It's looking like I'm in more of a murder mystery now than a romance. Or maybe I'm in both. It's all very exciting, plus a little bit creepy. CREEPY/ EXCITING! I wonder how much I actually look like her.

Tried to read but couldn't concentrate. Kept thinking about those books my mom used to read, the ones that always had a cover of some dark looming house and a young blonde woman running away from it, wearing a nightgown. Gothic thrillers. On our vacations Mom could read about two a day. I want to tell her now that I'm living in one of those books. And I just did, whispering it. I don't pray but sometimes I talk with my mother, tell her what's happening in my life. Tell her I'm living in one of those novels she used to like, and it's only a matter of time before I'm fleeing this house in my pajama bottoms and my UCLA T-shirt.

Nighttime now and I am too tired to explain everything I learned tonight. There are LOTS of people who believe that Adam killed that girl at the end of the summer, including the police. That's what E told me. And she also said that Adam was on-and-off involved with the girl and that he was the last one to see her that night and the only reason he hadn't been arrested was because he had an alibi, another girl in the village, but now that girl was looking pretty unreliable. Emma seemed really worried, and I felt bad about being excited and making jokes in this diary about being in a murder mystery. A girl was killed, and Adam had been seeing her. I wonder if E thinks he actually did it? I mean, he couldn't have, right?

Must sleep!

December 22

In bed and I'm staying here because it's so cold in this room. I woke to a scratching at my door and let the orange cat in. He is now sleeping on the edge of the bed that is closest to the radiator, which clunks and hisses but doesn't produce any discernible heat.

I am thinking about that murdered girl and Adam and everything that I've learned since arriving here at Starvewood Hall. Last night there was a more formal dinner in the dining room, about twelve of us around the table, including a friend and client of E's father, a man who had driven down from London. Mr. Chapman is some kind of entertainment lawyer, and the man at the table—he was only introduced to me as Daniel—is a bestselling author of spy novels, apparently. The two of them dominated the conversation. Daniel, in particular, was very funny and very handsome and I noticed that whenever he made everyone at the table laugh he would dart his eyes toward me to gauge my reaction. Dinner started with a mushroom soup and it was all I could do to not lick the bowl. Then there were duck breasts, and

I was pretty sure mine was undercooked and I was panicking a little about eating enough of it so that I didn't look rude, but I was saved by one of the dogs, who nuzzled me under the table. I successfully transferred most of my dinner to his jaws while the table was laughing at another one of the writer's stories.

By the time dessert arrived—something called trifle—I was involved in a one-on-one conversation with E, who had drunk a shitload of wine. That was when I heard more about her being worried that Adam was somehow going to be arrested because of his involvement with the murdered girl. Even though everyone at the table was talking, E was a little loud and her father noticed and interrupted her, saying something like, Emma, why don't you tell us all what you learned at university this autumn? I watched the blood drain from her face but then she moved her shoulders back and she talked about how she was falling more in love with the Italian Renaissance. Everyone went quiet at the table as her father began to grill her, asking for specific artists she loved, and what exactly was it about them, and finally catching her in a mistake about Raphael, and then looking very pleased with himself. I thought he was done but then he said, aloud, that his daughter wasn't quite pretty enough to also be stupid, and that was when Daniel, the writer, saved the day by standing up to make a toast to his hosts. I joined him and made a small awkward speech of my own, about how amazing it was to be taken in by a family halfway around the world. The faces around the table stared blankly at me so I kept speaking, and as I said the words, I was simultaneously aware that I would eventually spend countless hours replaying them with horror in my own head. After sitting back down I was hoping someone else would make a toast so I wouldn't be the last. It was Emma who came to the rescue, standing up with her wine, and saying how much she'd been thinking of her grandmother, who had died over the summer, how Christmas just wasn't the same without her. The whole table seemed moved, even Emma's terrifying father.

After dinner I found E out in the back garden smoking a cigarette and I joined her. You okay? I asked, and she looked confused for a moment, then said, Oh, my father, you mean. That was nothing. I suspect you'll see a far more impressive display during your week here. Cruelty is his gift.

Later, we were reading in the parlor when Adam came in, called E the ugly art historian (said as an affectionate, supportive joke), and said that he needed a word. The two of them went off, but I stuck around, getting talked into a game of Clue (called Cluedo here for some inexplicable reason) with Phoebe and Maggie and Uncle Simon, who, it turns out, is a sweetheart. He took the game very seriously, acting out all his lines, and making us all laugh. In case you were wondering, it was Colonel Mustard with the rope in the conservatory. After the game I hung around but E never returned and neither did Adam.

I went to the kitchen and found Daniel, the writer, making himself a sandwich. He seemed very pleased to see me, and the two of us sat at the large island and ate cheddar sandwiches and drank some red wine. When I told him that I should go to bed he put his hand on my thigh and asked me outright if I wanted to go to his bedroom instead. He's about twice my age and I was a little shocked but his hand felt nice on my thigh and I almost said yes. Instead, I got flustered, told him I was seeing someone, and made my way out of the kitchen and up the dark back stairs to my room. Now I'm wondering if I should have just gone with him to his room (a room that in all probability must be warmer than mine). The truth is that I have a crush on Adam or otherwise maybe I would have done it. I did tell myself way back in September that my year in London was going to be the year I made mistakes, and maybe Daniel the writer was a mistake I should have made. Besides, would Adam even have known? More importantly, would he have cared?

Back in my room, late afternoon. Wind rattling the window. E is asleep next to me, snoring a little, but I am wide awake and have only just managed to extract you, Dear D, from the bedside table and now I am occupying a tiny sliver of this bed and trying to not wake E up.

A lot has happened today but two things have happened that seem IMPORTANT. The first is that Adam had some sort of showdown with his father this morning and now he has returned to London. It was after breakfast. I was late as usual and while I was eating my toast with jam I heard a door slam somewhere in the house, and then Mrs. Chapman popped her head into the dining room, looking very pale and concerned. All she saw in there was me, alone at the breakfast table, reading Bonfire of the Vanities. Her head disappeared. Later, Emma told me that Adam had had it out with their father over breakfast, telling him that if he tried to humiliate anyone else during this week he would leave forever and never come back. According to E her dad said something along the lines of, If you left, then at least the town murder rate wouldn't rise again. I asked her if her father actually thinks Adam's a killer and she said, I don't know what my father *thinks but I do know that it wouldn't particularly bother him if he was. Sometimes I think he's a psychopath. My father, I mean. You don't think that he . . . I said. Killed that girl, E said, and laughed. Um, no, he IS interested in women but not in killing them, and then she laughed more, even though what she said wasn't funny.*

We took a short walk, E and I, and she told me stories about how cruel her father could be, and how her mother never really did anything about it, and how Adam was always threatening to stop coming back home for the holidays. It was starting to spit rain a little and we turned around. When we got back to the house, Adam was leaning up against his car smoking a cigarette (I don't know why I always mention that he's smoking a cigarette—I should mention it if he isn't). Anyway, he told us his bag was packed and he was fucking off back to London. Come back on Christmas Day, E said, sounding like a little girl. He asked her why and she said so he wouldn't be alone, and he laughed. Then he asked us both to come with him, that the three of us could bar hop our way through London over the holidays, and I was secretly hoping that E would be into the idea. But she scoffed at him. We can do that anytime, she said. He shrugged and got into his tiny car and before he drove off, he looked at me (first time he'd looked at me that morning) and said that he'd left something for me in my bedroom.

E seemed very upset about Adam leaving and dragged me with her to find her mother. All I wanted to do, of course, was race to my room to find out what Adam had left me, but for some reason E wanted me by her side. We found her mother in the glassed-in greenhouse (Oh my God, it's a conservatory, just like in

Clue!) at the back of the house, sitting on a wicker chair and making what looked like a list. I stood stupidly next to Emma while they had it out.

E: *Adam left.*

Mrs. C: *Yes, I'm aware of that, Emma. He told me before he told you.*

E: *Did you try to stop him?*

Mrs. C: *I told him I thought he should stay. But he's like your father, you know, once he's made a decision . . .*

E: *That's the only way he's like Daddy. Daddy's the reason he's leaving.*

At this point E was starting to sound like a little girl again and I was wondering why I was even in the room.

Mrs. C: *I'm not sure what Adam expected. Your father is your father, and he's not going to change.*

E: *I don't know how you put up with him.*

Mrs. C: *Well, I'm not prepared to have this conversation again. Your father has provided for me and for you and Adam. And in exchange for that he says and does exactly what he wants at all times.*

E: *You could defend us, you know, Mummy? That's all Adam and I ever wanted.*

Mrs. C: *How do you know I don't defend you all the time?*

That was essentially the end of the conversation although they repeated it in slightly different words two more times. I considered slowly backing out of the room but Emma was near tears and I didn't want to make it worse. One thing about spending time with Emma's SCARY family is that I feel less bad now about not having my own.

After we finally left the conservatory, E said, Right, there's no other choice but to get pissed and stay pissed for the rest of the week. Let's go to the pub.

I agreed and that gave me a chance to go to my room and change. On my unmade bed was a poorly wrapped present in green tissue paper. Scrawled in red ink on a white notecard were the words OPEN BEFORE CHRISTMAS. It was a white scarf, a very nice one (cashmere!), and of course I remembered his finger touching my cold skin below my throat, when he chastised me for not having a scarf of my own.

I wrapped the scarf around my neck and sat for a minute imagining Adam picking it out, touching it with his beautiful fingers. I said a little prayer (good luck with that!) that he'd come back before Christmas Day.

The pub was a bit of a blur, filled with people from the village (young and old) and E knew all of them. I wish I had time to say more about the hours we spent there—just for the future memory banks I'll mention Dorothy, about to turn a hundred, buying a drink for everyone, and E pointing out the boy she lost her virginity to (he saw her and fled) and how we laughed so hard with the two boys from Lower Clevemoor that I peed in my jeans a little. It was like a party in the middle of the day. The first half hour or so crawls by, everyone struggling to make small talk, then all of a

*sudden you realize three hours have passed, and it is dusk outside
and the man next to you is singing "The Holly and the Ivy."*

*At some point I lost E, and the girl who cleared the glasses
from the tables at the pub told me that she thought she'd gone
home. I got my coat and stepped outside. The sky was the color
of a bad bruise and light flakes of snow swirled in the cold air. I
didn't know what to do. Had E really gone home without me?
Finally I decided to return to the house as well. It was only a
five-minute walk, along the lane and then down the long driveway, and if E wasn't home then I could always return to the pub.*

*I wrapped my new scarf tightly around my neck, kissing it
and hoping no one saw, then began to walk, the wind behind
me, shoving me along. I'd done this walk enough to know that
the fastest route was taking the path through the woods that cut
diagonally to Starvewood Hall, but no way was I going to walk
through the woods all by myself (I am living in a GOTHIC
THRILLER after all). So I kept going along the road, almost
as dark as the woods, until I got to the gate that led down to the
manor house, turning onto the gravel driveway. I was halfway to
the house when I saw the man come out of the woods. It was getting dark but I could tell he was wearing a flannel coat and some
sort of cap. I stared at him, trying to make out his face, thinking
it was very white and very large, and then I realized he had a
large white beard, like Santa Claus. He stopped and just stared
at me, and for a moment, we were looking at each other, me kind
of hoping he might wave or do something friendly. But instead he
lifted a finger and swept it across his neck, then pointed at me.
It was all I could do to not run the rest of the way to the house.
I walked fast, however, turning around once and he was gone.*

Back in the house, trying to get my breath back, I wondered if I'd imagined him there. Then I decided I hadn't, and that I was very glad I'd decided to not walk through the woods. Even thinking about it made it feel as though I'd been stabbed in the chest with an icicle.

Mrs. Chapman passed through the hallway while I was taking off my muddy boots and asked me if I'd seen Emma. I told her, No, I was just about to look for her myself, she'd left the pub without telling me. And then I just kept talking at her because that's what I do. SHUT UP, I kept yelling inside my head.

When you find her, Mrs. C said, pretty much having to yell over me, tell her I need to talk with her. I don't know why I didn't immediately tell her that I'd seen a creepy guy outside, but I guess I panicked. For all I know he's just some local person, or maybe I was imagining it, or maybe Mrs. C would think I was just some crazy American trying to get attention. Or maybe I've seen a ghost out by the woods and I am in a GHOST STORY.

I went straight to E's bedroom, knocked on the door. There was no answer so I pushed the door open and she wasn't in there. I began to get a little worried, thinking about the creepy man I'd seen by the woods. I went back downstairs, looking through all the rooms, although not going near Mr. Chapman's study or the conservatory, hoping to avoid the scary parents. In the parlor I found Uncle Simon and his family, three of the kids playing a board game I didn't recognize, and Simon and Jeremy playing chess. I asked them if they'd seen Emma and they hadn't. In the library I ran into Daniel, the writer who'd tried to seduce me, and I could actually feel my cheeks turn red the moment I saw him. He must have seen it too because he laughed, then said, No hard feelings about last night, I hope, and I started apologizing to him. Stupid, I know, but it's my default mode, and I managed to stop long enough to ask him if he'd seen Emma and he said, No, as well.

Finally, I thought, screw it, heading to the conservatory to look for E's mother. I had decided to tell her that I'd seen someone suspicious, that that was the smart thing to do, but she wasn't there. At this point my feet in the damp socks were very cold and I decided that I should at least go to my room for my slippers. And that was where I found Emma, huddled up under the blankets on my bed.

She woke up briefly when I came in. So drunk, so cold, she said, and I got in next to her. She really was cold, her hands like ice, her torso shivering, and I cozied up to her.

You left me alone in the pub, I said.

Sorry, E said. I had one of those drunk moments, you know, one minute you're standing there cheerfully blabbing away, and then the room was spinning and I suddenly needed to get the hell out of there. I'm sorry, but you looked pretty happy with that bearded boy and I didn't want to make you leave with me.

Me: *How did you get home?*
E: *I walked, of course.*
Me: *Through the woods?*
E: *God, no. Not by myself. Why?*

I told her about seeing the man on the edge of the woods, and how he'd done that thing to make it look like he wanted to slit my throat, and she made me describe him. She thought for a moment, and then said that maybe it was the gardener who lived at the Rutherford house, how she was pretty sure he had a white beard and that he was probably just completely pissed. She kept yawning while she talked so I let her fall back asleep. Even though I'd had so much to drink I was wide awake. I quietly managed to extract you, Diary, from my bedside drawer, and write all this down.

December 23

A quiet day today although it is not over yet. It was a quiet night, as well, last night. Daniel took over the festivities and went out to get Indian takeaway for everyone, then rolled the television into the parlor so that we could all watch a videotape he'd brought of a film called Dead of Night. It's mostly horror but it's also Christmas-y, he promised, but even though I liked it, it was a stretch to call it a Christmas movie. Still, a perfect evening, everyone hungover, eating too much Indian food, getting cozy. Daniel barely looked at me and definitely didn't hit on me. It wasn't unfriendly, really, just that I think he'd moved me into the she's-not-going-to-have-sex-with-me category. He was reading me correctly, too, because I couldn't stop thinking about Adam. Every time someone came into the room from outside it took all my willpower to not turn around and see if it was HIM returning from London, striding in in his long coat, having changed his mind.

He didn't, of course.

And after the movie I went upstairs and fell almost immediately asleep, trying not to think about that figure emerging from the woods in the dusk, and what it might mean.

This morning I woke early and lay in bed, thinking about Emma and Adam. Thinking about the whole Chapman family, really. Have I been invited here as a buffer? Probably, but I'm not sure that bothers me.

I do feel close to Emma right now. We didn't start out that way, Dear D, as you know. There was that whole love triangle (more like a LIKE triangle) with Stuart Montgomery back in late September, but E and I talked that out two nights ago in front of the fire with the Baileys. She told me that she thought I did her an enormous favor by hooking up with Stuart even though she'd confessed to me she liked him. She said I'd saved her heartache and annoyance. It was a relief to hear that, even though I'd already assumed that I'd been forgiven somewhat. I'd been invited to her house, after all.

After eating a breakfast of cold toast and jam I wandered the quiet house. Ever since Adam left I can't stop thinking about him. And I can't stop thinking about Joanna Davies, either, the girl who was murdered at the end of the summer. Was Adam more involved with her than he'd let on? It seems clear that maybe he was, and it seems clear that some people in the village believe he murdered her. I went back upstairs, walking quietly past Emma's door, stopping in front of Adam's bedroom. I would never have gone in, but the door was slightly ajar and when I pressed my hand to it, it swung open silently on its hinges.

*I stepped inside, telling myself that I was just there to look at his bookcase, since I needed something new to read (*Bonfire of the Vanities *was just not cutting it). His room was messy but charming. Above his single bed he'd pinned up a poster of An*

American Werewolf in London. *In one corner of the room he'd left a pile of discarded clothes—rumpled jeans, T-shirts, and a pair of striped boxer shorts on top. It was all I could do to not touch them (or steal them, if I'm being honest). I did step closer to take a look, imagining the way he'd look wearing boxers and nothing else, and then the whole pile shifted as the orange cat emerged from under it and raced from the room. I came out of my shoes, and have no idea how I didn't scream, but somehow I didn't. I looked through his books while my heart attempted to restart. He has a lot of children's books—Tintin, Roald Dahl, Asterix and Obelix—and a few adult books, mostly Ian Fleming novels and Stephen Kings, plus a few Martin Amis books. I grabbed a copy of* Perfume, *since I've been meaning to read it (Nicola said I should), and it felt good in my hands, knowing that Adam had held it as well. But it also felt like a good excuse if someone suddenly came into the room, that I was just there to borrow a book.*

Before I left I went over to his messy desk, on top of which was a stack of econ textbooks, plus one framed photograph— Adam with a pretty blonde girl. At first I wondered if it was Joanna Davies but I picked it up and realized it was Emma, a picture from a few years earlier. Adam looked just like Adam but E looked different, her hair sprayed and teased, and she was wearing a lime green top and stonewashed jeans. Adam wore a white Oxford shirt, its collar frayed, and dark trousers, and he was posing as though it was the last thing he wanted to do, his shirt untucked on one side. The two of them were standing in front of a twisted tree in what looked like a park. I put the picture back down, suddenly feeling as though I'd looked at something I shouldn't have, even though it was just a picture of a brother and sister.

Before leaving Adam's bedroom I peered into his closet, being hit with the musty smell of unwashed clothes. Half of the clothes were piled on the floor of the closet but there were shirts and blazers hanging on the rod. I ran my hand along them, all that soft cotton that had spent time next to his skin, and then my fingers detected some slippery fabric. It was a pale dress, the size a young teen might wear. I pulled it out. It seemed handmade, its label with Emma's name on it, and I wondered why Adam was keeping it in his closet. There were brown crusty stains down the front of the dress and I had a sudden flash of memory, Emma at the beginning of the term getting a nosebleed at the Dragon and telling everyone that she used to get them all the time. Had she wrecked this dress with a nosebleed? And if so, why was it in Adam's closet?

The radiator in the room clunked loudly and I jumped again, deciding that I should get out of Adam's bedroom before someone saw me.

It was bright outside, and I couldn't find E, so I decided to go for a walk into the village. It was an excuse to wrap Adam's scarf around my neck. Once I was outside it was impossible not to think about the man with the large white face I'd seen by the woods, so I walked along the driveway and then the road, relieved when I reached the village, other people about because the weather was so nice. I browsed through a charity shop that had used clothing, then thought about going into a tearoom with steamed-up *windows, but when I opened the door I saw how crowded it was inside and quickly abandoned that plan. I was starting to walk back to Starvewood Hall when I felt a tap on my shoulder and turned around to see that it was the dark-haired girl from the pub who had been talking with E. She said, I thought that was you, and reminded me her name was Sophie, said she saw me nearly come into the tearoom and then leave.*

We talked for a while on the street. She was super friendly, which was strange because she'd barely acknowledged me at the pub. She seemed kind of amazed that I'd been invited to spend an entire week at the Chapmans' house, and just talking to her was making me feel guilty, like I never should have accepted the invite, like I wasn't quite worthy of it. I kept trying to end the conversation, but she kept asking me more questions, and then saying how she wished the Sheepfold was open so we could get a proper drink. Right before I got away, she said, That was weird, wasn't it, what happened in the pub when Joanna Davies's mother stared at you?

Do I actually look like Joanna? I said.

You really do, Sophie said, making the word really *sound like* rally.

Me: *Strange.*

Sophie: *Spitting image, honestly, except for how skinny she was. It's funny because everyone used to say how Jo looked like Emma, because they do, sort of, I guess, but you, you could actually be her.*

Me: *What was she like?*

S: *Oh, I suppose you'd say she was a very local girl, like who knows if she'd even ever been to London, except for maybe on a school trip. I don't mean to sound like a snob or anything, but it's just the way it is. And that's why we were all surprised when we heard she was going out with Adam Chapman.*

Me: *Isn't Adam a local boy?*

S: *I mean, not really. Yes, of course, he grew up here, but his parents have a flat in London, and it's not like he went to the local school or anything. Jo's father is an electrician and her mother used to work up in the big hotel in Cheltenham.*

Me: *Were they serious, Adam and Joanna?*

Sophie laughed. *At least Adam wasn't. I can't speak for Joanna, obviously. Adam probably had three girlfriends in London at the same time he was with Joanna here in Clevemoor. She was just someone for when he came back here, I guess, in case he got bored, or in case Claud wasn't around.*

Me: *Who's Claud?*

S: *Claudia's another local girl, but more like Emma and me and not like Joanna, if you know what I mean. Her parents have the house up on the other side of the Sheepfold, up the lane, I forget what it's called. Anyway, her and Adam have pretty much been on and off for three years or so. He was with her,* *or that's what she says, the night that Joanna got her head bashed in.*

Me: *(and by the way, I'm getting very interested now) What do you mean "That's what she says"?*

S: *Oh, just that I guess it's all falling apart, her story. Honestly, I've known Claud my whole life and she's sweet but she's really, really dumb. (Rally, rally.) It's a surprise because her father's some kind of advertising genius and I heard that her mother wrote a book about local history or something. But Claud, like I said—not the sharpest tool. She told the police that she was with Adam all night but I guess it's now turned out that she had dinner with her parents at a pub in Bourton on the Water earlier so that means that Adam's alibi is totally shot.*

Me: *You don't actually think he did it?*

S: *Did what? Bash Joanna Davies's head in with a rock? God, no. He's a bit of a prick but he's not a serial killer or anything. I just think he probably told her to meet him out by the Chapman cottage and then he forgot or whatever and some pervert came along and did her in.*

Me: *What's the Chapman cottage?*

S: *It's that old stone cottage behind the house you're staying in. Everyone round here calls it the Chapman cottage because its where the kids too young to get into the pubs go. I mean, it is kind of famous so it wouldn't surprise me if some pervs already hang around there, waiting to see the fifth formers come stumbling out. I'm sure that's who Joanna ran into, some rapist or something. But now everyone is saying that Adam could get done for it.*

We talked some more but my hand is aching I'm writing so fast and the rest of what we talked about wasn't that important.

I got back to Starvewood Hall and had lunch with E and her mother at the big table in the kitchen. Turned out they'd spent the morning shopping in Oxford, leaving after their breakfast. They seemed to be getting along okay even though they were both quiet. Lunch was fish and when I was squeezing my lemon the juice hit E right in the eye, and that made us all laugh. After we'd all eaten, Mrs. C said she was going to lie down for a while, and E asked me what I wanted to do. When I told her I was happy to read she looked a little relieved and said she'd read as well. We both went to the library and I got back into Perfume *(every time I flick a page over I think of Adam's hands doing the same thing), while E flipped through her Caravaggio book. I like* Perfume *even though it's making me crazily aware of how everything smells. I must have fallen asleep while reading it because I had the dream I always have, the one where I can't find my mother's hospital room and I know she's dying and no one will tell me where she is, only this time it's the smell of the hospital I notice the most, the smell of sickness and flowers and rubbing alcohol. My nostrils were filled with it when I woke up, and my neck was sweaty and E was no longer in the room.*

I looked out the lead-paned window and it was starting to get dark outside and I had this sudden crazy urge to go look at the cottage down by the pond. The one that girl Sophie was talking about. I bundled up and went out through the empty conservatory.

I don't know what I expected but the cottage was pretty run-down. The walls were made of stone and seemed sturdy, but

the roof was covered with moss and bowed in, like it might col-
lapse at any moment. I pushed open the door. Inside was just
one big room, the floors made of stone and covered with cigarette
butts. There was a big fireplace filled with ash and broken glass.
The mantelpiece was completely covered with melted candle wax.
There were a few chairs scattered about, mostly wooden except for
one, upholstered in old red velvet, the seat split open, white stuff-
ing coming out of it. The whole place made my chest hurt, and I
couldn't imagine people wanting to be there at all. But maybe I'd
have been into it when I was fifteen and there was nowhere else
to go. I guess it's like that parking lot at the abandoned Howard
Johnson's that we all used to hang out at. I walked back up the
gentle slope of the yard to the warm house.

I started to get a bad feeling about this week.

Chance of romance: nonexistent.

Chance of gothic thriller murder mystery: growing by the
minute.

Dear Diary! Dear beautiful romantic Diary! I need to sleep
but first I have to tell you that I just had dinner at . . . oh, now
I've forgotten the name of it, some glorious hotel about a half
hour drive away. It was like something from a fairytale—cozy,
dark, everything decorated with twinkling lights and garlands. E
came and got me at dinnertime and told me to put on my best
dress, that she was treating me to a proper dinner in a hotel and
that there'd be a surprise. I just thought she was going to give
me a gift or something but when we got to the hotel and were
having predinner drinks in the bar, in came Adam! He had his
long coat on, and a green pill-covered sweater that he managed

to make adorable. He was with some other cute boy, and they'd both driven down from London to meet us. We drank a flock of wine and Adam's friend was very funny (not nearly so beautiful as Adam) and the food was SO good. Cheese soufflé, mushroom wellington (best ever), and sticky toffee pudding.

Walking back to our cars there was actual snow in the air, swirling around like in a snowglobe, and E and the other boy disappeared. Then it was Adam and me, and he said, You're wearing my scarf, touching it. And then we were kissing and it was like the most perfect kiss I've ever had, his hand on my neck, and the perfect amount of tongue, and honestly my legs were weak. He moved his hand down to my hip and, seriously, not to be gross or anything, but I wanted him to touch me between my legs so bad I was almost groaning. I think I would have let him do it to me right there and then if he'd wanted to. But he stopped kissing me because E and the friend were back—BOO, HISS!—and they'd bought ciggies at the hotel bar and passed them all around and I just wanted to be alone again with Adam. Before we all got back into our cars, I asked him if he was going to come back to Starvewood. He said that he wouldn't but that it was killing him because I was there. He laughed a little after saying it because it sounded corny, like a bad novel, and then we all said goodbye.

Am I in love with Adam?

December 24

Christmas Eve morning. Still in bed. There are little frost lines on the window and I just read what I wrote last night. Honestly it seems like a dream. The beautiful hotel—I remember the name now, it was the Green Man—and the kiss with Adam in the snow.

I must have had too much to drink because I barely remember the ride back to the house with E. She was quiet, and I was babbling drunkenly, although about what I have no idea, and I kept wondering if she'd seen me kissing Adam. She must have, right? But she didn't bring it up, and I didn't dare bring it up. Adam is amazing but I don't want to ruin my friendship with E.

It's so cold in this room and I need to pee.

Back in bed now. I got up, pulled a sweater over my nightgown, and snuck down the hallway to a bathroom that was somehow, impossibly, colder than my bedroom. I peed then drank as much water as I could straight from the tap. The house was quiet and instead of coming immediately back to my room I walked to the portion of the house where the family slept and slipped into Adam's room. It was dark in there, the curtains drawn, and I stood for a moment to let my eyes adjust, and that was when I saw the figure under the covers shift. A string of thoughts entered my mind. It must be Adam! He had decided to come back here after our kiss last night. He wants to be with me! But then the figure was sitting up and I saw long blondish hair and heard a girl clear her throat and I quickly backed out of the room just as I saw Emma's face.

Why did I run? I suppose I was embarrassed but now it's so much worse because I snuck out of the room. UGH! Maybe E didn't see me. She looked groggy and confused, and like I said, the room was pretty dark. But even so, she must have known someone was in the room. Should I just confess everything to her? Tell her that Adam kissed me, and that I went into his room just to feel close to him? And then what? She'll probably freak out and ask me to leave. I don't know what to do, and my head is pounding. At least the orange cat is back, knocking his head against mine, purring like a revving engine.

I can't stay in bed all day. I'll get up and go downstairs and tell Emma everything. More later, Dearest D.

It's four in the afternoon and the police have just left after questioning Emma and me. This all started just before lunch. We were in the kitchen, E and me, plus E's aunt Judy and two of E's cousins. We were helping them make lunch—ham and leek pies—and it was NOT going well. The cousins were making a mess of everything and their mother was losing it, drinking wine and yelling at them both, which only made them laugh more. E and I were kind of enjoying the show. (By the way, I haven't said anything to E yet about the incident in Adam's bedroom because she hasn't mentioned it either. For all I know she's embarrassed as well for being caught sleeping there. Why was she sleeping there anyway? Maybe his room is warmer?) So Aunt Judy, who isn't helping really, just panicking, suddenly realizes that the house is out of milk entirely. Emma offers to go down to the village to see if the grocers is open. I offer to go too, but Aunt Judy asks me to stay and help cut up carrots, so E runs off.

Phoebe and Maggie really are helpless. They are trying to make puff pastry, reading a recipe book, and I'm not sure they know what they're doing. Not that I'd know how to make any kind of dough so I'm pretty happy that my job is vegetable chopper. It's fun, and

Aunt Judy is either starting to relax or getting fairly drunk at this point. There's a radio in the kitchen and the station is playing Christmas songs. When it's time to make the gravy, Aunt Judy is stressed again because E isn't back with the milk. It's been like forever so I walk to the front door and open it, looking out at the gray day, the bare trees moving in the cold wind. I stand there for a while, just staring out, waiting for E, and then I see her, running as fast as she can across the front yard, coming diagonally toward the door. I can see her face and she looks terrified, and I step out onto the damp stone steps in my socks. E is looking over her shoulder like someone is chasing her but there's no one there. When she reaches me she is so out of breath that she can't talk, and she wraps her arms around me, starting to sob.

When she is able to speak, she tells us that she was chased in the woods by a small man and that she thinks he was the same man that I saw a couple of days ago. Emma's mother calls the police and when they arrive we all go to the living room and sit down. Emma tells the whole story.

She'd walked into the village along the road and bought milk at the pub. It was cold out so she decided to take the shortcut back through the woods even though she had a strange feeling like she was either being watched or followed. When she'd been walking in the woods for just a little bit she heard a stick break behind her and turned around. She said there was a man, his coat flapping, running at full speed down the path in her direction. She thought he had something in his hand, like maybe a rock, and she said his face was very pale, and with a white and bushy beard. She turned and ran as fast as she could, not daring to look back, but saying that she could hear footsteps behind her, getting closer and closer, and it was only when she emerged from the woods onto the front lawn of Starvewood Hall that she didn't hear them anymore. She could see me waiting for her on the front steps and kept running.

You said he was small, one of the policemen said. There are two of them, both young and dim-looking.

He looked small to me, and fast, but I don't really know, E said.

That was when I said that I had seen him too, and all the eyes in the room went to me. I told them about my walk back from the pub and how he'd been standing at the edge of the woods watching me, and that I'd been scared.

Why were you scared? the less dim of the policemen asked me.

There was something wrong-looking about him, I said, like he was wearing a disguise.

Policeman: *A fake beard?*

Me: *I guess so. It looked too white somehow.*

P: *Was it a Father Christmas beard?*

Me: *Maybe. But the man wearing it wasn't fat, or wearing red, or anything like that. I mean, I never thought I was seeing Santa Claus at the edge of the woods.*

The conversation kept going like this for a while. Emma was calming down, and her mother brought tea for all of us, including the two young policemen. I was beginning to think they were delaying leaving because it was warm in the house and Emma's so pretty. Right when it looked like they were going to leave, the gong of the doorbell sounded and Mrs. C went to answer it. Another policeman came in, a middle-aged man, and he was holding a plastic mask by its edges, one of those cheap molded masks with a rubber band around the back to hold it in place. I knew as soon as I saw it that it was what I'd seen that creepy man wearing. And it actually was a Santa mask, sort of old-fashioned-looking, the skin as white as his beard, and with a little plug-shaped nose and cut-out eyes. Emma gasped when she saw it and started to nod. And I started nodding too.

The policeman had found it in the woods, along the trail that led from the Sheepfold pub to Starvewood Hall. Emma, a little bit hysterical, asked them if they were going to dust it for fingerprints.

All three policemen looked kind of sheepish, and the older one said, Don't you think it's probably just some kid playing a prank?

Then Emma went off, saying how a girl had been killed just three months ago and all the police were doing was figuring out ways to pin it on her brother when there was probably a maniac living in the woods. She was very haughty when she said it and it was the first time I'd noticed that there was a resemblance between her and her mother. Anyway, the attitude must have worked because before the policemen left they promised that they would look into it.

After they were gone and we all calmed down a little, E and I spent time in front of the fire. I asked her if she really thought that the person who chased her in the woods was the person who had killed Joanna Davies.

I don't know, she said. But what bothers me the most is that they are all convinced that Adam did it and that's why they don't take this seriously. And then she said something like, I know Adam as well as I know myself and he's not a killer. He might be a prick, but he wouldn't kill anyone.

It was exactly what Sophie had said, and I asked, What do you mean, a prick?

E: *I don't mean a prick, exactly. I mean, he's not a particularly nice person. He's selfish and conceited, but he's not a killer. He doesn't beat people to death with rocks.*

My heart started to pound because I knew I was about to make a confession. I said, I have a huge crush on Adam.

I don't know what I expected—like maybe she'd kick me out of the house or slap me in the face—but instead she kind of half laughed and said, Of course you do. Everyone has a crush on my brother.

I must have looked hurt because she leaned forward and said, I don't mean . . . I mean maybe he does as well.

I said, It doesn't sound like you think there's much hope.

E: *Has he shown any interest in you?*

I told her about the kiss and how he'd bought the scarf for me, and I could tell that she was thinking about what to say to me. After a moment, she finally said, Then I guess maybe he's changed. Deep down, he's a good guy. I've always known that.

Me: *You really think so?*

E: *(looking all thoughtful) There is no one I know better than Adam, and, if I'm being honest, he sometimes sees the world as his playground, just like my father and all his creepy friends do. He can be selfish and hurtful and it's all about him, but he's also unbelievably loyal. If he loves you, he will look out for you.*

Then she told a story about how she had been traumatized by an ex-boyfriend when she was sixteen and how Adam took care of everything.

He spoke to the boy, E said, which was great, but he also ended up sitting with me for three nights straight because I was having trouble sleeping. Neither of my parents would do that. He's not like them. He's a good person.

We stayed by the fire for a while, until it got too warm. I told E that I was going to go up to my room for a while before the evening began (I really wanted to get to you, Dearest, and tell you everything about today), and when I was starting to move, E stopped me and said, kind of nervously:

I don't even know if I should tell you this, but Adam is going to be at the Sheepfold tonight.

Me: *He's coming back for Christmas?*

E: *No, just to the pub. He's driving back down with Tony and then I think both of them are going to stay at some friend's house.*

Me: *Are we going?*

I must have looked and sounded like a lunatic because E put her hand on my knee the way you'd put a hand on someone to calm them down, and said, I don't know. I mean, whoever was chasing me this morning is still out there.

Me: *Oh, right. I'm sorry. I forgot.*

E: *I suppose we could go, the two of us, if we promise to stick together the whole time, and if we don't take the path through the woods.*

Me: *Really?*

E: *Maybe. Let's see. I can't promise anything.*

And now I'm in my room, my fingers literally crossed, dreaming of seeing Adam tonight.

I must have dozed off because I just had the strangest dream. I was wandering through this house, from room to room, and no one else was here. I went into Adam's room—somehow I knew it was his room even though it didn't look like his real room, at all, but more like a cave. I opened his closet door but his clothes weren't in there, just dresses like the one I found, all covered with blood. And then I was walking down the upstairs hall, except that it was so long I couldn't even see the end of it. I turned into Emma and Adam's parents' room, where there was a huge ornate bed, and beside it was a small dirty mat, covered with tiny bones, like chicken bones, and somehow I knew that Mr. Chapman slept in the bed and Mrs. Chapman slept on the mat. I was going to go downstairs but when I got to the top of the stairs I could see that a party was happening on the first floor, people milling about silently all dressed in black dresses and tuxedos, and that I wasn't invited. I stood for a long time, scared to move in case someone saw me on the balcony, but then I realized that everyone could see me, everyone was looking up. Emma and her whole family. My Renaissance tutor from the Courtauld Institute. My high school guidance counselor Danny. My mother was there, also in a fancy gown. But I was looking for Adam and they were all looking right back at me, frozen, in their party clothes, drinks in their hands. I wanted to back away so they couldn't see me—I wanted to flee the house entirely—but my legs wouldn't move. And then the party was starting again, as though they actually hadn't seen me at all. And I woke up.

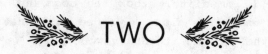

TWO

That was the last entry in the diary, followed by fifty or so white pages. Tucked in toward the back of the diary was a newspaper article that I had clipped and saved. It is yellowed and worn now. Two pictures accompany the article. One is of a police detective, obscured by fog, standing in the woods where the murder happened. The other is a photograph of me, a snapshot provided by my mother from when I was sixteen, on holiday in Greece.

BRUTAL MURDER ON CHRISTMAS EVE

TWO LONDON STUDENTS ATTACKED RETURNING FROM FESTIVE NIGHT OUT AT COTSWOLD PUB

After leaving the venerable Sheepfold Pub in rural Clevemoor, two female students currently studying at the Courtauld Institute in London were brutally attacked. American Ashley Smith died on the scene, while Clevemoor resident Emma Chapman remains in critical condition.

"It was my son who first realized they were

missing," said Simon Chapman, uncle of Emma Chapman. "I immediately took the dogs out and we found the girls along a wooded path that leads from the pub back to Starvewood Hall. We didn't know that they'd gone to the pub."

The unknown assailant lay in wait along the well-trodden path, striking both women with what appears to be a heavy rock. The blood-soaked scene of the crime is being minutely investigated for any evidence.

Det. Chief Supt. Dennis Marley, who is leading inquiries, described the murder and assault as "particularly vicious and horrendous. There is evidence to suggest, however, that the two women fought back against the monster who did this." Both victims received multiple wounds around the neck and head areas. There was no suggestion of sexual interference.

Ashley Smith, originally from Sacramento, California, and Emma Chapman, a Clevemoor resident, were staying at Starvewood Hall, the long-time country residence of Roger and Alison Chapman, parents of Emma. Roger Chapman QC is senior barrister at Woodstone Chambers, a leading firm in the media and entertainment field. The students of art history had been spending the Christmas holidays in this idyllic Cotswold village.

"I've known Emma since she was a child," said Ruth Barnard, who has worked at the Sheepfold for twenty years. "The whole Chapman family have been coming down here since I first started employment here. I've watched Emma grow up into a lovely young woman. I'm shocked with what's happening in this village right now."

This is not the first murder to blight this

part of the world. In September, eighteen-year-old Clevemoor resident Joanna Davies was found bludgeoned to death on property behind the Chapman house. The death is still under investigation.

Det. Chief Supt. Marley would only say that the police were considering all possibilities in their investigation. "I ask that the public remain vigilant to a continued threat in the area, while not immediately jumping to conclusions. We will solve this case."

I killed Ashley Smith that Christmas Eve. This was back when I was called Emma Chapman.

It was after a large family dinner with my parents and Uncle Simon and Aunt Judy and their kids, when Ashley told me she'd thought about it, and that we absolutely had to go to the Sheepfold to see Adam and Tony. She was almost frantic, so in love with Adam, already. I'd never really doubted that he could do it, that he could make Ashley so enamored that she'd be willing to go out at night even with a maniac on the loose, but he'd smirked and told me that it was not going to be a problem. And it hadn't been.

We snuck out of the house just as Uncle Simon was organizing a game of Trivial Pursuit. It was cold that night but cloudless, so everything was lit with a silvery moonlight. We'd linked arms, Ashley and I, and walked quickly to the pub. I honestly don't think Ashley was that scared to be out at night because she was so excited to see Adam. It occurred to me that I could get it over with right then and there, alone on the path to the Sheepfold, but I decided it would be better to do it on the way home. For one thing, Ashley would be drunk and that would make it that much easier. And the other thing was what Adam kept insisting. "If we're going to do this, Emma, then let's make sure that Ashley's last few days are good ones. A little Christmas cheer, a little romance, a couple of good snogs. Least we can do, right?"

It's strange rereading her diary. Somewhere between what Ashley wrote and my own memories of those few days lies a resemblance to the truth. To this day, I don't really remember lying in front of the fire with Ashley and drinking Baileys. I have no doubt it happened but it's a blank spot. I do recall the drunken afternoon in the pub and the dinner at the Green Man with a fair amount of clarity. But I also remember that on Ashley's first full day at Starvewood Hall I gave her a tour of the grounds, showing her the cottage down by the pond. At least I think I did, and it bothers me that she doesn't mention it in her diary. Maybe it didn't happen.

The two strangest mentions in the diary are when Ashley wrote that she saw me sleeping in Adam's bed on that final morning. I have no recollection of that, and I can't imagine why I would leave the comfort of my own room to sleep on Adam's smelly sheets. The other unsettling moment is when Ashley describes her dream, saying how she saw a mat with bones on it beside my parents' bed. The thing is, my father did use to make Mummy sleep on the floor beside the bed. It was a way of punishing her. I asked her about it when I was just a child, and Mummy lied and said that she preferred sleeping on the floor, because sometimes Daddy wanted the whole bed to himself. But that was something that happened when Adam and I were little kids. So how did Ashley dream of such a thing?

Should I tell the whole story now, how it's coming back to me, the end of that terrible year? I did always tell myself that killing that American girl was the only way to save Adam (maybe me as well) and that I would never pretend it didn't happen. I wouldn't erase the memory.

Let's go back, shall we? The truth of it is that when I first heard Joanna Davies had been murdered out behind the cottage I immediately thought of Adam. That August I'd gone to France with Mummy to visit her old school friend Patricia. Adam had stayed behind, claiming a sudden interest in gentleman farming, which meant that he was drinking with Sam Barley and John Dawkins. I knew he was seeing both Joanna Davies and Claudia Gowan. He'd been with Claudia for years, but Joanna was a new thing, and I'd told him earlier that she was going to be trouble.

"Explain trouble?" he'd said, and I told him the story of how Joanna had been dumped back when she was twelve years old by Alan Hunter and she'd snuck into his room and peed on his bed.

"Seriously?" Adam said, a wide grin on his face, clearly more amused than concerned.

So when Mummy told me over breakfast that a) a new out-of-town supermarket was opening in Stow ("There goes the Cotswolds") and b) Joanna Davies ("poor thing") had been found dead on our property, a current of fear ran through my body. I knew that Adam had done it. I thought that he'd probably been provoked, not that that would have mattered. He'd taken a life.

It was not a complete surprise. Adam and I are twins. I knew him as well as I knew myself. He was brilliantly funny, but had a dark side. At the age of six he told me that he hated both our parents. Even then we both lived in fear of our father, but I still loved our mother. I asked him why he hated both of them, and he said he hated Father because he was cruel, but that he hated Mother more because she was weak. Then he told me, "When Father decides to kill us both, Mummy won't stop him. She'll probably help because he'll make her."

"How will she help?" I asked, suddenly terrified that Adam knew what he was talking about.

"She'll hold us still while Father slits our throats."

"But we're their children," I said.

"They only had us because it's what you're supposed to do to be a family," Adam said back.

I sort of believed him. Although we were the same age, he often seemed older.

When we were nine, he became fascinated with animals, deciding that he wanted to be a veterinarian. He had a pet rabbit named Myra that he doted on all summer. A few days before the two of us were to leave for our respective boarding schools, Adam told me that Myra had died. "I wasn't going to leave her here with our parents," he said. "She's better off now."

Later, before he buried her in our pet cemetery in the

woods behind Mother's herb garden, Adam dissected Myra in his room, using a steak knife.

"But she was your pet," I said to him.

"She was my pet when she was alive. Now she's dead it makes sense that I would take a look at her insides. I'm going to be a vet, remember?"

I did know that blood didn't bother him. In fact, he was fond of it. I knew this because when we were a little older, I wrecked my favorite dress with one of those nosebleeds I used to get all the time, and when I told him that I was going to throw it out, he asked me if he could have it. We were thirteen then. I asked him why and he shrugged and said he liked the look of blood. "It changes color after a while. At first, it's bright red and then it turns brown, like the color of dirt. Blood ages."

It was around this time that I asked my brother if he thought he was a bad guy. We'd watched *Dial M for Murder* on television with Mummy, who loved Alfred Hitchcock movies, and for some reason that movie had scared me more than any monster movie I'd ever seen. Maybe it was because the man who plots to kill his wife is just an ordinary man. What I mean is that he looked like an ordinary man. He was played by Ray Milland in the film (Grace Kelly was the pretty American wife) and I thought that he looked like my father. He didn't really—I know that now—but Ray Milland wore nice suits and had a posh haircut and was always standing at the drinks tray to see if anyone wanted a whiskey, and all those things made me think of Daddy at the time.

"What do you mean, a bad guy?" my brother said.

"Like in that movie we watched. Are you like the husband who wants to kill his wife?"

"Oh, you want to know if I'm a murderer. If I'm someone who might like killing people?"

"I guess so," I said.

He thought for a while, then said, "Yes, I suppose I am like that man. I mean, it wouldn't bother me too much if I killed someone, but I would never really do it."

"Why not?"

"It would make Father way too pleased if I screwed up my life that badly. Can you imagine? Plus, I don't think I'd like prison very much."

When I returned from France, Adam was still at Starve-wood Hall. The police had questioned him—twice, he said—but he'd been with Claudia on the night of the murder. "Were you really?" I asked him, the first time we were alone. Adam and I were not as close as we had once been, but I knew he wouldn't lie to me.

"You know Claud," he said. "She'll do anything for me."

"What are you saying?"

We were in his room. I remember the window was open and Adam was smoking, tapping his ashes into a coffee mug he kept on the sill. He shrugged.

"Oh, Adam," I said. "You actually killed her. You killed Joanna."

He blinked rapidly, then said, "I didn't mean to do it, Em. I'd been trying to break it off with her for weeks and she was driving me crazy. The thing is, the thing about Joanna, was that she was a little bit kinky. I think she enjoyed it when I hurt her."

"You mean physically?"

"No. What she really enjoyed was me telling her how disgusting she was and how I was lowering myself to be with her."

"God," I said. "Did you like that too?"

"I did, at first, a bit, but then I realized I was starting to feel a little too much kinship with Father. The night it happened, the night she died, I was honestly trying to leave her, Em. I'd successfully broken it off, at least I thought I had, and left her at her house. I'd told her I didn't want to see her again at all, that we were done. But, later, when I was back here in my room I heard rattling on the window and she was out there in the garden, hurling pebbles at the house. I didn't want her to wake up everyone so I went out there to talk to her. We went behind the cottage, to the edge of the pond, and she was crazy, just out of her mind. She told me that she'd only let me break up with her if I did something really despicable, like hit her. That otherwise she'd just keep trying to win me back."

I must have looked skeptical because Adam said, "I'm telling the truth. You know I don't lie to you."

"I know," I said.

"So I agreed to hit her. At first I just kind of popped her one in the nose and she laughed and said it didn't count. So then I punched her harder, but not even that hard, Em, and she went straight down on her back. And that's when she banged her head on a rock."

"She was dead?"

"Oh, yeah. Instantly. I almost decided, right then, to just go to the police and confess everything. I mean, honestly, the whole thing was a misadventure. But then I thought of our parents and I just couldn't handle how they'd react to it. So I bashed her a few times in the face with a rock just to cover up the fact that I'd hit her, and then I hightailed it to Claud's place, and got her to agree that I'd been there all night. I mean, it's holding up. Claud, at this point, doesn't even think she's lying about it."

"What do you mean?"

"I mean she actually believes we were hanging out all that night. She's suggestible, that Claud, which is a nice way of putting it, I guess."

"What did you do with the rock?" I said.

"I threw it into the middle of the pond."

I thought the whole thing was going to go away, but by the middle of September, Adam told me that the alibi was falling apart. We'd met up in London, at the student union pub, and Adam actually looked a bit scared. "Claud's been caught lying about that night, telling the police that she'd had dinner with me when she'd actually had dinner with her parents at some pub. It's killing me because all she really had to do was say that I came over after she got back and hung out with her in the guesthouse, which is practically the whole truth. Anyway, I have a very bad feeling. They're dragging the pond and I don't know if they'll find the rock or if it'll have blood on it or anything. I mean, do blood and fingerprints stay on a rock that's been underwater? I don't even know."

"I don't think so, Ad. I wouldn't worry about it."

"There's another thing," he said.

"What?"

"I was seen that night, going from our house over to Claud's. You know Garry Wishaw, right?"

"I think so."

"He's at the Sheepfold every night."

"Oh, right. Always needs a shave. Stares directly at your tits when you talk to him."

"He doesn't stare at my tits, Em, but, yes, that's him. I bumped into him, like almost literally bumped into him, on that path on the other side of the pub."

"Was he pissed?"

"Of course he was. Legless. But if they talk to him, and if he even remembers, it's just more evidence that points to me."

The pub was filling up, and I told him we should talk about something else. We started a game we'd been playing since we were children, studying strangers and telling each other what they were like. Only this time it was more fun because I knew most of the kids in the Dragon and I could tell Adam if he was right or wrong.

Ashley Smith was there that night. Adam spotted her right away because he said, "Oh my God, the ghost of Joanna Davies just walked in."

"That's Ashley. She's an American here for the year. You'd like her, she's emotionally damaged."

"Is she?"

"Well, I've only talked with her a couple of times, but

according to my friend Iris she was raised by just her mother and then her mother died when she was in high school."

"Good lord. She's an orphan. And she's American, you said?"

"She's from California, and, yes, I guess she's technically an orphan. If she were rich, she'd be a Henry James character. I shouldn't be making fun of her, it's sad."

We didn't talk any more about Ashley until right before she left. I'd gotten distracted because Stuart Montgomery had come in, had one quick drink with Adam and me, and then joined a group of his rugby friends at another table. I told Adam how much I was crushing on him, and he said, "I can leave, you know."

"No, please don't. I'm playing the long game with him."

About an hour later, Adam said, "I think your American friend is playing the short game."

"What do you mean?"

"Look."

Stuart Montgomery was leaving the pub, Ashley Smith hanging on to his arm, bumping her hip against him as they walked. "That bitch," I said.

"I thought she was tragic."

"You know, I actually told her that I liked Stuart Montgomery. Last time we were here in the Dragon. I can't believe she's leaving with him."

"You should kill her," Adam said. This was the type of comment he made all the time, but I hadn't heard him say something like it since the incident with Joanna Davies. I must have given him a look because he said, "Kidding, obviously. And, yes, in very poor taste."

But two days later, Adam came to my flat after he'd been out with friends. He was drunk (as drunk as he ever really got, which wasn't much), and he told me that he was now convinced he was going to spend the rest of his life in prison.

"What have you heard?"

"I was out with Nick, and you know how he's studying criminal law?"

"I guess so."

"He told me they've started testing for DNA at crime sites. It's this new thing and it's basically going to mean that no one gets away with anything at all."

"What do you mean?"

Adam did that annoying thing he used to do, when I didn't immediately understand something. He spoke slowly, and said, "You are aware that all humans have this thing called DNA? And it's unique in every one of us, just like fingerprints?"

"Uh huh," I said.

"So apparently we're just shedding the stuff all the time. Bits of skin, saliva, hair. And so pretty soon they'll know exactly who killed everybody because of the stuff."

"But if they were going to do it with Joanna Davies wouldn't they already have tested?"

"They've already taken samples of everything, it's just a matter of looking at the DNA. I punched her in the face. It was skin on skin, and my DNA is probably all over her. That's the kind of thing they can look at now."

"Just relax. They're not coming for you tonight."

"Maybe I should just run away, go to Thailand or something and become a barman."

"If you disappear then you can't come back. It will essentially be an admission of guilt."

"I know," he said. "The truth is, I don't want to live somewhere else. It's terribly boring but I love England and I even love Clevemoor. The thought of never being able to come back here is . . ."

I got him some tea and we sat on opposite ends of my velvet sofa. We pressed our feet together, both of us having to raise our legs to do it. We used to sit that way all the time when we were young.

"I actually *have* devised a plan that will completely exonerate me," Adam said, a smile back on his face.

"Oh, yeah. What's that?"

"Well, it involves you, Em."

"Okay."

"And your friend from America."

"Who's that?"

"That girl you pointed out to me at your uni pub. The tragic orphan who stole your boyfriend right out from under you."

"Ashley Smith?"

"Yes, how could I have forgotten that name? Are you ready for my brilliant plan?"

"You seem very pleased with yourself all of a sudden."

"That's because my plan is brilliant even though I know you'll never do it. That's why I can talk about it. Ready?"

I shrugged. Adam said, "First, you become friends with

Ashley Smith, close friends. I know that won't be hard for you because you have at least some of the Chapman charm. Then you invite her to visit Starvewood Hall. She's an American. She'll think she's gone to cozy Cotswold heaven. And then you simply kill her, Em. Hit her on the head while she's out rambling. And I'll be in London with a rock-solid alibi. Suddenly the police will be looking for the Cotswold serial killer, and I'll be eliminated from the investigation."

"They'll be looking for a brother-sister killing duo, more like," I said.

"Highly doubtful. You see, you'll be attacked too, bopped in the head with a rock. And you'll be able to describe the attack."

"You really have actually thought about this."

"I guess so," Adam said, his face shrouded by the steam from his tea.

"I know you want to tell me the whole plan, so just go ahead. I'm not going to do it obviously, but I'll listen."

"Okay. So, you know how I said you'd bring her to the country any old week? I actually think this will work best over Christmas."

"Won't you be there?"

"Let me talk. I will be there at the beginning, long enough to provide Ashley with a bit of romance toward the end of her life. I see your expression and I'm ignoring it for now. It will come in handy, you'll see. We'll get Ashley Smith out to Starvewood Hall four or five days before Christmas. I'll be there at the beginning, but then I'll leave early to return to London."

"Before Christmas?" I said.

"Look, I'll leave because one of our parents will say something so awful and unforgivable that it will make perfect sense for me to leave. I'll just claim I can't take it anymore. Trust me, you know there'll be a moment. So then I'll be gone and it will just be you and Ashley. The two of you will be traipsing back and forth between the house and the Sheepfold, like we always do that week. And here's the brilliant part. At some point, you'll have to make sure that you're out alone in the woods or something, and while you're there you can say you got chased by someone. They'll believe you, Em. You're a good actress.

"Now keep listening. It won't just be you who sees the crazy stalker in the woods. At some point, if we can arrange it, we'll make sure Ashley sees someone spooky as well. She doesn't have to be chased or anything, just a witness. So when you claim you saw this person she'll jump in and say she saw them too. All this will be reported directly to the police."

"So if Jack the Ripper's running around in the woods," I said, "why would we go back out to the pub? Why would we leave the safety of the house?"

"Because you'll tell Ashley that I'll be there, that I've come down from London for a drink and she'll be dying to see me. This will be on Christmas Eve, or whatever works. You'll go together. I won't be there because I'll be in London surrounded by reliable, sober witnesses. And that's when you'll do it, Em, on the way back from the Sheepfold. Make it look like you were both attacked, and that Ashley died and you lived."

"And you'll be a free man."

"Yes, that's the most important part."

"And I'll go to prison for the rest of my life."

"Not a chance. They'll never suspect you."

"What about all this DNA evidence you're talking about?"

"But you'll be there too. You'll pick up a very big rock, bop Ashley on the head, down she goes, then bop yourself as hard as you can without causing any real damage, and down you go. There won't be someone else's DNA on it, but they'll just assume that your attacker wore gloves. Then you'll run to the police with your story, and it will all be backed up by the fact you were chased through the woods the day before, and by the fact that Ashley saw someone too. And, of course, by the fact that the killer will have already struck, killing Joanna Davies back in September."

"Okay," I said. "It's time for me to go to bed. Do you want to stay here or can you make it home?"

"You don't like my plan?" He was smiling broadly, enjoying himself.

"What, your plan where I commit premeditated murder to cover for your accidental murder? No, I don't like it."

He did spend the night on the sofa but was gone by the time I woke up. This was sometime in October, and I'm not sure I can properly explain how, by December, I had decided that I was willing to move forward with this plan to murder Ashley Smith. I'll try to explain, though, if only for myself.

There were two main factors. The first was that I'd heard from my friend Sophie, working hard to be the most-informed gossip in Clevemoor, and she told me that her brother was friends with a local policeman and that they were all convinced of Adam's guilt, that it was just a matter of finding a solid piece of evidence that placed Adam at the scene of the crime. The second factor was that I really had quite liked Stuart Montgomery, and watching Ashley march him past my table at the pub had irked me no end. I couldn't help but feel she had done it on purpose. The phrase that kept ringing through my head was that Ashley Smith had drawn first blood.

No, that's not really fair, even though at the time I did use it as a justification.

I did what I did for Adam. We were born into a bad family, raised in a house where we didn't feel safe. We only had each other. And I knew that if the situation were reversed, if Adam needed to kill someone in order to help me, he wouldn't hesitate. And that was why I agreed to do it. Adam was going to go to prison unless we did something about it. There was never any doubt about that. And I've learned to live with my decision.

I found out randomly that Ashley Smith was not going back to America for the Christmas break. It was early December and at this point I'd managed to become friends with her, not close friends, exactly, but close enough that an invite to join my family and me for Christmas break would not seem entirely out of the ordinary. One night a group of us were out at a pub in Russell Square when another American student from the Courtauld Institute told me that Ashley wasn't going home for Christmas.

"Why not?" I said.

"She has no family there. You do know that it was just her and her mom, and her mom died."

"Yeah, I knew that."

I must have rolled my eyes a little because Stephanie, the student I was talking to, said, "Yeah, she likes to make sure everyone knows how sad her life is. But, honestly, it *is* totally sad. I told her she could come back with me to Connecticut and spend Christmas with my dysfunctional family, but she said she was looking forward to being in London. I don't know, sounds depressing to me."

It's funny. I remember inviting Ashley to come and stay at Starvewood Hall a lot earlier than December 17. But according to her diary, I did wait that long. I must have been putting it off, still not sure if I could go through with the plan. It's kind of a wonder that no one else invited her home for Christmas, but then again, she was a loud American, talking all the time. Other students didn't dislike her, but she wasn't exactly popular. A little of her went a long way.

Adam, meanwhile, had worked out the plan down to every minute detail. He was the one who would pick her up at the train station, thus ensuring that he could lay the foundation for their romance. I'd continued to ask him why it was so important that she fell for him, and he'd insisted that it was the only way to ensure that Ashley would come with me down to the pub on Christmas Eve. "Remember, at this point you'll have been chased by a maniac in a Father Christmas mask through the woods and Ashley will have either been chased too or at the very least will have seen this person.

You'll both be scared to go out. We need something to lure her to the Sheepfold."

"And that will be you?"

"Yes, I'll be the bait."

"And you're sure that you'll be so irresistible that she'll risk it all to come see you?"

He'd raised an eyebrow at me and shrugged. We were brother and sister and he'd never pretended any kind of false modesty in front of me.

"There's another thing," he said. "These are going to be Ashley Smith's last days. Let's at least make them enjoyable and memorable."

"We're inviting her to our family home. How enjoyable do you think that will possibly be?"

"She'll love it. We'll just make sure she doesn't wind up alone with Father or one of his friends behind a closed door, or in a one-on-one conversation with Mummy. We'll take her over to that inn in Fareham and buy her a great fucking dinner. We'll get her gifts and I'll pour on the charm. She'll get a whole lifetime in a week. Jesus, Em, we'll be doing her a favor."

I've thought about Adam's words quite a bit over the years. He did buy her a beautiful scarf, and he did kiss her in the snow. Maybe he really did it all sincerely, a way to make her sacrifice less painful. But sometimes I watch Elspeth, my aging cat, who has twice caught a mouse and batted it around on the kitchen tiles before killing it, and I wonder if Adam was simply playing with his prey while she was still alive.

Regardless, Ashley was very thankful to be invited somewhere for Christmas, and she did have a good time while she was there. Rereading her diary, it all comes back to me, at least the parts I remember. That crazy afternoon at the Sheep-fold. That lovely pub dinner at the Green Man when Adam came back with his friend Tony. It even seemed as though she enjoyed some of the creepier moments of her visit, like the appearance of the maniac in the mask (me, of course), and being questioned by the police. It was all part of the Gothic thriller–ness of it all. And it turns out she even had a pretty bold proposition from Daniel Parkinson, that lecherous nov-elist friend of Father's. That might have changed everything, if she'd agreed to sleep with him. Maybe she would have fallen in love with him instead of Adam. I should look him up, Daniel Parkinson, sometime. He's probably dead by now, like Mummy and my father.

Ashley really did fall for my brother, which was not a sur-prise at all. The pervy novelist never stood a chance. I remem-ber watching it happen, watching Ashley's eyes follow Adam across a room, search for him whenever we'd enter the pub or the parlor. At the time I treated it as proof of the weakness of her character, telling myself she was just a slutty American girl who would throw herself at any handsome English boy with an accent. It wasn't fair, but I was also steeling myself for what I had to do. I spent that particular Christmas alternating between fits of terror and moments of excitement. More than excitement, really. It was the electric thrill that only comes from truly transgressive acts. I was playing with Ashley, as well, pulling her closer to me so that I could kill her in such a way that no one would ever suspect I'd had anything to do with it. I felt all-powerful and sick to my stomach at the same time.

In the diary, Ashley mentions several times that I talked with her about my parents, and about Adam, but I don't really remember any of that. I must have, though, because everything she has me saying—talking about how cruelty was my father's gift—was spot on. But I just don't remember it. I don't even remember telling her the story about Leo Dennis, the boy who humiliated me the summer before my last year at school, and how Adam had dealt with him (I don't know the specifics of what he did, but I do know that Leo practically disappeared off the face of the earth). I do remember Adam staying with me for several days, when I felt like I might have a breakdown. So I must have told all this to Ashley, even though all I remember is her doing the talking, all that non-stop chatter delivered in her Valley girl accent. I do remember sleeping in her bed that afternoon she found me there. Adam and I had decided it was imperative that Ashley saw the man in the mask at some point, that she be a witness to the random maniac that we were conjuring up out of thin air. The mask was something that Adam had found in a gutter in London the year before, after some sort of Christmas rave. The long tweed jacket and the cap I'd bought at a charity shop a few villages over, and we'd hid them all in the hollow tree in the woods that we'd both known about since childhood. The first night that Ashley stayed over at Starvewood Hall, I actually went out after everyone was in bed and got into the outfit, then stood outside in the moonlight on a patch of the back garden that could only be seen from Ashley's room. I snapped a few branches, hoping she might hear them and look out her window and see me, but I don't think she ever did. She certainly didn't mention anything other than strange noises in her diary.

That left our drunken afternoon in the pub. I departed first, changing into the outfit in the woods, then hiding in the thick of the trees to wait for her to pass by. After a little while it occurred to me that if she was coming back from the Sheepfold alone, she might go the long way, down the road and then the driveway. I moved to the edge of the woods, where I could keep an eye on both the path and the driveway. I was frozen and cursing my brother's name for making me do this, while at the same time feeling rather clever.

Ashley did come down the driveway eventually. I stepped out onto the lawn, praying she'd turn to see me. She did, when she was about halfway down the driveway, and I stood there, staring at her, feeling ridiculous and exposed, as though later on she'd come up to me and say, "Why were you outside by the woods in that child's mask?" But, then, because she was staring I suddenly found myself sliding a finger across my throat, and then she was hurrying to the house and I knew that I'd frightened her. I went back into the woods and changed out of my disguise then ran to the house myself, entering through the conservatory and taking the back stairs, where I got into Ashley's bed, hoping she'd gone looking for me everywhere else but her own room. When she found me, I pretended to be very drunk and very cold and she kept me warm.

For some reason I remember being nervous at this point.

Maybe it had something to do with how ridiculous I'd felt in the large tweed coat and the mask, that it felt so obvious that Ashley would know it was me. I kept waiting for her to say something like "I know it was you. I know you only brought me out here to murder me and save your brother. It's totally obvious."

Of course, she didn't say those words because it never occurred to her. I think that was the real reason I was scared. Once I'd put on the mask and fooled Ashley it had become real. I was really going to go ahead and commit this murder. The die was cast, as they say.

After that I didn't need the mask or the clothes. I had only ever needed them just the once, so that Ashley would see me and be able to describe what I looked like. On the day that I pretended that I'd been chased through the woods by a small man with a white beard I buried the jacket and the cap underneath the neighbors' rotting compost pile, then left the mask, wiped free of prints, along the path in a place that I hoped was obvious enough for even a local policeman to discover.

It all went so smoothly. The police came out on Christmas Eve and took all sorts of notes about this mysterious stranger who had been spotted by both me and my guest. And, as Adam had predicted, the fact that Ashley was now in love with my brother meant I didn't even have to talk her into leaving the house after dark to visit the Sheepfold. She was longing to go. Adam wasn't going to be there, of course. He was spending Christmas Eve back in London at his friend Tony's family's house. There would be several witnesses this time, reliable ones.

I remember how excited Ashley was that night. It was actually a nice evening, all around. Mummy had made her salmon en croute, which she always made for Christmas Eve, and had managed not to dry it out. Father had a crisis with one of his clients, an actor being sued for breach of contract or something, and was in and out of his office all evening. I think because he was gleefully yelling at people on the telephone meant that he didn't single out any members of his own family for abuse. There was laughter and lots of wine. It's funny how well I remember that particular meal—the salmon, the beetroot salad, Uncle Simon's kids all in their teens back then. How many dinner parties have I been to over the last thirty years that are now just completely erased from my memory?

After the party broke up, I was prepared to remind Ashley that Adam was going to be at the Sheepfold, but it wasn't necessary. She cornered me, her face flushed and her eyes bright, and asked when we were going. We made a plan to meet by the back entrance in twenty minutes and sneak out into the night. I somehow doubted that anyone would stop us despite the convincing case I'd made that a maniac was on the loose. I mostly wanted to avoid my cousin Jeremy, who definitely would have wanted to come along, or even Uncle Simon, who might have offered to escort us there and back. But my entire clan had settled in front of the television to watch *A Christmas Carol*, and Ashley and I went out the back. We took the driveway instead of the path through the woods and I remember Ashley saying that we should have weapons with us.

"Like what?" I said.

She picked up the largest rock she could find from the edge of the driveway, and I thought to myself that she was making this so easy for me, that I should pick up my own rock and hit her with it right then and there. But for some reason it seemed imperative that we go to the pub first, that people see us there, and that we should get attacked on the way home. We kept walking, Ashley holding the rock the whole way.

The Sheepfold was lovely that night, the fire roaring, a pot of mulled wine on the bar next to a warming tray of free sausages. A group of carolers stopped by and sang "Good King Wenceslas" and "In the Bleak Midwinter." Through all this, Ashley could not keep her eyes from the front door, waiting for Adam to stride in like some romance novel hero. He never came, of course, and I like to think that despite that, Ashley had a nice last evening. Is that heartless of me? Or is it the opposite? I'm not sure anymore. I do believe that if Ashley Smith hadn't died that night, Adam would have eventually been identified as Joanna Davies's killer and he would have gone to prison for the rest of his days. And I would have been there with him, as well, the way I was always with him, no matter how far he was from me.

Just before the pub closed, I convinced Ashley that Adam was not going to show. She was very drunk by this point, slurring her words and unable to speak of anything but Adam. She kept repeating the same line again and again: "Emma, say the word and I won't go near him again. I promise." I knew she was lying. Adam had worked his considerable charm on her, and she was in deep. I remember thinking that by killing

Ashley that particular night I was at least going to save her the heartbreak of having fallen in love with my brother.

It was far colder outside than it had felt during our walk to the pub. Darker too: clouds massing in the sky and obliterating the moon and the stars. I easily convinced Ashley that we should take the shortcut through the woods. "It's the two of us," I said. "We'll carry rocks and walk really fast. We'll be fine."

I'd brought a torch with me, a small pen-shaped one, and I handed it to Ashley so she could lead the way. She was laughing as she walked, stumbling forward with each step, the illumination from the small penlight bouncing around in front of her. In the pub I'd felt nervous and edgy about what I had to do, but now that we were in the woods, a calm had come over me. *Calm* is maybe not the right word. It was a sense of purpose. And it was something else, something colder. It was pure focus, all my mind and body prepared for this one task.

The rock I had in my gloved hand was almost too large to hold. Adam had told me many times that I needed to hit her with a heavy rock, or else I'd simply hurt her. "You're taller than her by a little," he'd said, "so that will help, but just don't hesitate. Give it your all with the first strike."

I told her to slow down, then placed my left hand on her shoulder. "Point your light straight down the path," I said. And as she did I brought the weighty rock down on the crown of her head as hard as I could. She made a sound halfway between a groan and an expulsion of air, then dropped to the ground in a heap. I knelt beside her and hit her two more times in the face. One of her legs kicked, and then she was still. Blood pooled on the cold, hard forest floor.

I'd thought a lot about what I needed to do next. I lay down next to Ashley and pulled her close to me, as though I'd been trying to shield her body at one point. Her own blood now covered one side of my face and the shoulder of my jacket. I stood up and transferred the rock to my left hand, put my right hand in front of my face and struck awkwardly at my knuckles, grazing them enough to draw blood. Then switching the rock back to my right hand I struck myself in the face, up near my temple, grazing it. I felt blood trickle down my cheek. It wasn't enough, though, and I knew it. Adam and I had talked about this in detail, and he'd said that I wouldn't be able to sufficiently hit myself. "It's the same way you can't really tickle yourself, isn't it?"

I stood on the path, Ashley's body on the ground beneath me, and threw the rock straight up in the air. It came down on my shoulder, my down-filled parka thick enough that I barely felt it. So I did it again, hurling the rock high up in the air, and turning my face up toward its tumbling descent, moving a little bit at the last moment so that it would strike me along my cheek.

The next thing I remembered was one of Mummy's dogs licking at my face, and the sound of voices. I could easily have died out there, but my cousin Jeremy, bored on Christmas Eve, had gone looking for someone to raid the drinks cabinet with, and when he couldn't find either Ashley or me, he alerted his father, who became concerned. Simon was smart enough to realize we'd most likely gone to the pub, but by then it was forty-five minutes past closing time, so he bundled up, took both his sons and all the dogs, and went to look for us.

I don't remember too much about the hours after we were found. The rock had knocked me unconscious and had also opened up a sizable gash on my right temple. Ashley and I were carried out of the woods by my uncle and his sons, a decision that no doubt infuriated the forensic team brought in to examine the scene. Ambulances were called. I was taken to Cirencester Hospital, although I have no memory of getting there. I came back into consciousness the following day, my memory impaired, my face throbbing underneath thick bandages. In my initial plan I had decided that I would describe the attack—the walk back from the pub, the figure in the mask lurking in the woods—and that I'd somehow managed to fight him off by picking up the same rock he'd used to attack us. I would tell them it was all a haze. But what I told them in the hospital was that I had almost no memory at all of the attack, that I only really remembered leaving the pub and deciding to take the shortcut through the woods.

I had been in the hospital for twenty-four hours when Mummy broke the news that my friend Ashley Smith had perished in the attack.

When I was finally released, after undergoing plastic surgery for my facial lacerations, I made one more taped statement for the police, in preparation for the official inquest. I told the same story, and while telling it I looked into the eyes of my interrogators and saw not even a shred of distrust. Afterward, one of the patrol officers, whom Ashley had called dim-looking in her diary, brought me a cup of tea and told me how lucky I was to survive. I cried real tears.

I WON'T RECOUNT THE NEXT TWO YEARS OF MY CONTINUED education in London, except to say that they were unpleasant years at best. The last time Adam and I talked about Ashley Smith was at a crowded pub in Charing Cross, when he whispered in my ear that I had saved his life. Needless to say, the perpetrator was never caught, but they did stop considering Adam a prime suspect, just as he'd known they would. The Cotswold Killer became a tabloid sensation for a while, and since I was the girl who'd survived the second attack, I was flooded with requests for interviews or simply statements. I refused them all. But I always felt the eyes on me at university functions and at student pubs. There was even a period when I was followed around by a troll-like journalist who would hide in bushes outside my flat, then leap out and take my photograph.

I had already decided that I was going to leave England for good as soon as I had my degree. I had no interest in ever seeing my parents again, especially since the death of my grandmother ensured that I now had money of my own. There had been a time when the thought of not seeing Adam again would have filled me with despair, but that time was now gone. Ever since I'd murdered Ashley Smith in order to ensure his freedom, we'd grown further apart. I was happy, I suppose, that he wasn't going to go to prison for the remainder of his life, but I could no longer bear to be near to him.

My initial plan was to move to Italy and study to be an art restorer, but as I was consolidating my possessions in preparation for the move, I was reminded that I still had a valid passport for Ashley Smith, along with her Californian driver's license, several of her credit cards, and, of course, her diary. Adam had managed to get to her diary before the police did, when he returned to Starvewood Hall on Christmas Day. Having reread it, I don't think there was enough in there to really point the finger at either Adam or me, but back then he was erring on the side of caution.

"To the victor goes the spoils," Adam said, when he gave me Ashley's possessions. I'd expected to see his wolfish smile, but he looked serious as he said it, almost proud.

I held on to the journal, and to all of Ashley's personal items. I wonder what the police thought about never finding her passport—I assume they must have searched her flat—but I never heard anything about it. She was a nineteen-year-old girl from America and I guess they figured her passport had gotten lost in the messiness of her life.

I remember staring at her driver's license photograph and her passport photo, both of which had been taken in 1986, when she'd been sixteen years old. She wore a fair amount of makeup in both pictures, and when I compared her pictures with photographs of myself from when I'd been the same age, I realized that we really did look alike. (And that we'd both looked like Joanna Davies.) I'd known this already, of course, that there was a superficial resemblance, but when she'd been alive that resemblance was so quickly obliterated by her accent and the way she carried herself, the way she gestured. I abandoned my plans to move to Italy and began to dream of moving to America instead.

I vividly remember the day at Heathrow Airport when I presented the American passport that said I was Rebecca Ashley Smith to the pimply officer at the boarding gate for my flight to New York City. I was so certain that a swarm of policemen would descend upon me, but all he did was stamp my passport and wave me through, never truly looking at me. And then the same thing happened at JFK International Airport six hours later. I had left my home country and been reborn as Rebecca Smith in America. And that is who I am today. And who I am happy to remain. I do not miss my family, and I do not really miss Adam. I live a rather charmed life in New York City, happily single, but with a network of generous friends. I fundraise for a well-endowed nonprofit.

I go whole weeks these days when I don't think about my family, or my life in England, or about my namesake, Ashley Smith. Years ago I began to holiday on an island in the Penobscot Bay of Maine, and it is there that I am most free; thoughts of my previous life don't seem to exist in that glorious region of New England. But there is no avoiding Christmas, especially in New York City. As the days get shorter, the department store windows light up with their annual displays, designed to lure the tourists; and the Christmas music is everywhere—at the doctor's office, at my corner bodega, at my favorite bookstore. There is no escaping the season, and I don't try to, except for my yearly refusal of all invites to other people's homes. I am content on my own. I have learned to live with what I've done, and Christmas is just a time when the reminders are more constant.

Before I put Ashley's diary back into my box of keepsakes, I flip through the pages once more, just staring at her looping cursive script, the exclamation points, the joy she seemed to feel at being alive. After Adam gave me the diary, I didn't read it right away. I considered burning it, probably the prudent thing to do, but in the end I held on to it, reading through the pages years later after I'd already established myself in my new country. Since then I've read it several times, always a little bit amazed by how different Ashley was on the page versus how she seemed to me in life. In person, I discounted her, saw her only as shallow and not particularly bright. Socially awkward and far too loud. Someone who laughed too hard at bad jokes and flirted too much with whatever boy happened to be in the room. But the truth is that I actually like the version of Ashley Smith that I found in her diary. She is quirkier, more perceptive, and more alive than I think I was back then. I suspect that, over time, her inner life would have begun to show itself more, that she would have shed some of her superficiality, gained some confidence. Or maybe I just like to think that.

Riffling through the pages I arrive at the start of the diary, her full name and the date at the top of the page, and then these words:

Starting a new diary because I am starting a new chapter in my life! London, here we come!

It's strange to sit here on this plane and know that over the next few months I will meet new people and experience new places and try new foods and I don't know what any of those things are yet. But they exist! They are sitting there waiting for me. I am trying very hard not to fantasize about what it will feel like, to just let it all happen. Still, I am picturing beautiful pubs, and foggy London streets, and cute boys in tweedy jackets. And I'm worried that because I'm picturing all these things they won't happen, and I'll wind up in some nasty part of the city, drinking Bud Lights at a college bar and hanging out with other American students. Oh well, if that's what happens, then that's what happens. At least I won't be in California.

The stewardess asked me in a very posh way if I wanted red or white wine with my meal and I tried to look as old as possible (do they card on airplanes?) and asked for white and now I have this adorable little bottle. Thank God for alcohol since I kind of hate flying. Except for the part where it takes you someplace entirely new. That part I love.

It's after dinner now and the lights are dark like I'm somehow expected to sleep. But I'm just getting more excited and am not remotely tired. I know I shouldn't do this but I want to jot down a quick list of rules for my trip:

1. *Don't fall in love with the first boy who's nice to you.*
2. *Being a vegetarian doesn't mean that you only eat pizza!*
3. *Drink a glass of water in between every alcoholic drink.*
4. *In museums, pick one piece of art and really look at it.*
5. *Keep up with this diary! (This shouldn't be too hard, I already love you, my dearest new bright white Diary.)*

6. *Well, I can't think of a sixth right now so I'll just say—Be yourself, Ashley! They can't take that away from you!*

I actually am a little sleepy all of a sudden so maybe I'll close my eyes. I'm thinking of you, Mom, like I always do. You told me once that life is short and I always think about that, as though you had a premonition about your own fate. You told me to have fun and be kind, and good things will happen. I know you would have been so excited that I was going to spend an entire year in London!

Ugh, turbulence!

I know that if I let myself I will keep reading, right up to the point where I invite Ashley for the Christmas holidays at Starvewood Hall, so I shut the diary and return it to the box in the closet, and tell myself that I had a moment of weakness and I shouldn't look at it again for years, at least.

I stand up, so fast that I am suddenly light-headed, then go to the window and peer outside. It is dark, and I can see that the roads are slushy with ice, but it doesn't appear to be sleeting anymore. I don my winter clothes and head out for a walk, desperate for some air. Howard the doorman holds up the bottle of Macallan 25 that I gifted him as I walk past, and I tell him to "Save some for me" as I hustle by and out onto the street.

There is a cold wind blowing down Seventh Avenue and the sidewalks are turning slick, but it feels good to be outside in the city and practically have it to myself. I walk several blocks, Christmas lights plastered everywhere, and enter a Chinese restaurant. The tables are filled with families, a tradition in the city, but the bar is empty, and I slide onto a stool and order a mai tai and the soup dumplings. I am there for about an hour and a half, long enough to order two more mai tais. The drinks are delicious, but they do not work; Ashley's words from her diary keep repeating in my mind, and eventually I decide to walk back to my apartment.

Howard's shift is over, otherwise I might have sat with him for a while, but, instead, I enter my apartment, and I am not surprised to find her there, my Christmas guest. It has been a few years, but reading the diary was probably what conjured her up. She hovers slightly above the floor, dressed in her winter clothes, her face caved in like the last time I saw her.

"Hi, Ashley," I say.

"Emma," she says. It's always strange to hear my old name. She is the only one who uses it now.

"Merry Christmas," she says. Her voice hasn't changed much, still too loud, as though she wants to make sure that she is being heard.

Elspeth pads in from the bedroom, looking at Ashley with wide eyes. I'd forgotten that Elspeth can see her too, although she treats her with the same regal disdain with which she treats all my guests.

"I've been thinking about you," I say.

"I know you have. I have the same thoughts you do. And I saw that you were reading my diary again."

After hanging up my coat and taking off my boots I walk across the living room, avoiding coming close to her, and get myself a glass of water in my alcove kitchen. I feel her eyes on me, even though she is quiet for a moment. I steel myself. She has come before, and she always stays through the night at least. In the past I've tried to fight her, or tried to flee, but it makes no difference.

I crawl into bed and she gets in there with me too. Elspeth, my regular bed companion, has chosen to sleep next to the radiator in the living room, the farthest point from where we are.

"How does it feel," Ashley asks me, "to still be alive?"

"Don't you remember?" I say. We've had this conversation before.

"I remember what it felt like to be nineteen and alive. I don't know what it feels like to be fifty and still alive."

"It feels different," I say. "When you're young you think there are so many possible roads, but when you're my age, you've been on the same road for a long time, and there's no getting off of it."

"It must be nice."

"Ha," I say, and watch as her one eye darkens. "No, it is nice," I continue, before she can say something else to me. "It's comforting, I suppose. There are fewer surprises at this age. Even seeing you is not too surprising."

She smiles, and I'd forgotten how horrible it is to see her smile. When her mouth opens so does her cheek. I haven't turned my bedside lamp out yet, but even so, the blood that spills from her face is not red, it's black, the color it was in the sporadic moonlight the night she died. She must see me looking at her wound, because she says, "Your face is almost completely healed now, but I can still see the scar."

"Can you?" I move my hair back to touch the ridge of bumpy skin.

And then she sings, which is worse somehow than seeing her smile. She sings Christmas carols—"The Holly and the Ivy" and "In the Bleak Midwinter" and "What Child Is This?"—and my nostrils fill with the smell of her death, and my brain fills with the tuneless words.

Just before dawn, as she begins to fade, she asks me the question I was hoping I wouldn't have to hear. "How is Adam?" she says.

"I haven't seen him for close to thirty years. But you know that already."

"But you feel him, don't you? You feel how he is?"

"Sometimes I think I do, and sometimes I'm not so sure."

"When was the last time you looked for news of his other girls? I know that you can do that now, even here from this apartment." She is speaking of the internet. Was that even a word back when we first knew each other?

I cannot lie to her because she always knows, so I say, "I haven't looked for a while."

"Maybe you should look tomorrow."

"Do you know something?" I say.

She smiles her terrible smile, and says, "I know everything."

Then she sings some more and is gone.

I stay in bed all of Boxing Day, unable to move. When Ashley comes to stay I am always left with a hangover so much worse than anything alcohol has ever done to me. I am hollowed out, empty of any emotion but fear and sadness. But on the following day I feel well enough to get out of bed. I go online and force my fingers to punch words into a search engine. First, I try *murder* and *unsolved* and *England* and there are too many hits so I start looking just at Yorkshire, and that is where I find what I hoped I wouldn't.

A twenty-two-year-old woman by the name of Galyna Stupkova was found battered to death in early October in the Dales. She'd been walking home from her job as a hotel receptionist to a house she shared with three other women from the Czech Republic, all working in the service industry. There are several pictures of her. She was blonde with a wide forehead and a slightly pointed chin, and she looked like Joanna Davies and Ashley Smith (and like me too, of course, when I was that age). She also looked like the other murdered women that I've read about over the past years, all found in various locations across the north of England. They are all young and blonde, and they are mostly foreign. They are never too close to Huddersfield, where Adam Chapman is now a Member of Parliament, but they are never too far away either. All these homicides are unsolved. Some journalists have tried to group these deaths together and say that there is a serial killer who preys on young blonde women. But it never quite sticks. Maybe because sometimes the victims are robbed, sometimes not, and once, one of the women had been sexually abused postmortem. The cause of death in all these murders is usually blunt force trauma to the head, but not always. And all the recent victims seemed to have led lives full of angry ex-boyfriends, expired visas, and drug problems—enough to suggest that their murderer was most

likely someone they knew. So far, their deaths remain unsolved. The police have refused to draw any links between
them, although one of the articles I've read suggested that
whoever was killing them was clever enough to change the
details of their deaths so that it wouldn't look like the act of
a serial killer. I remember a quote from the piece, something
like "Might this be the work of the cleverest serial killer in
British history?" I wonder if Adam read that piece too, and if
he was secretly pleased.

I half expect Ashley to appear again, hovering at my shoulder, but she is gone now. Not forever, of course, but for a year
at least.

She lingers, though, like she always does. I wake up some
mornings with memories of her in my dreams. Maybe because I want her to go away, and maybe because it's the right
thing to do, I find the email of the journalist who wrote the
piece that linked the recent crimes near Huddersfield. Her
name is Diya Advani, and one day in early January I create
a fake email account on a computer at the New York Public
Library and I write to her. One sentence. "Take a long, hard
look at Adam Chapman."

After typing those words I shut down the computer and
race to the library's restroom, where I lock myself in a stall
and throw up my meager breakfast.

Over the next month the Christmas decorations that fes-
tooned the city begin to come down. The days grow longer,
and I immerse myself in my work. My nonprofit raises money
for victims of violent crime, and while I am well aware that
my work does not make up for what I've done, and for what

my brother continues to do, I do know that it sometimes helps me sleep at night.

Sometime around late February, Christmas will have been entirely expunged from the island of Manhattan. I usually take note of the last seasonal object I see—often a sad and brittle tree nestled in among the garbage bags along the sidewalk. And then comes spring, with its hopefulness and flowers, and summer, all brightness and parties and weekend trips. Mid-August, I take my three-week vacation in Maine and return to Manhattan in early fall. I say fall, now, just like a true American. I actually think it's a good name for the season, the world coming back down to barren earth after the buoyancy of summer. And then there is Halloween, a holiday that seems to become more important every year for the younger residents of Manhattan, all those twenty-somethings with their ever-present cellphones and their fascination with dressing up. Sometime between Halloween and Thanksgiving is when I encounter the first sign that heralds the return of Christmas, usually some snatch of music in a pharmacy, or a television advertisement, or even sometimes a window display by an overly ambitious retailer.

By early December there is no refuge. Even in my office there are pine boughs decorating the reception desk and Richard, from the neighboring cubicle, has put up a 1950s pink tinsel tree that everyone finds hilarious. And it is here at the office, trying to ignore the season, that my life changes. I am scrolling through news stories from our appalling world, when I see that Adam Chapman, Huddersfield MP and mainstay of the Yorkshire smart set, has just been found dead at his family's manor house in Clevemoor. This story has followed closely on the heels of a report that he was a person of interest in a string of unsolved murders from the past thirty years. I read everything I can find on the story, going back through news archives. Two weeks ago, Diya Advani had broken the story that police had zeroed in on Adam Chapman as being potentially responsible for a number of unsolved homicides. I have to go on to a Reddit stream in order to discover that Adam shot himself with a hunting rifle in the cottage behind our family home.

I sit at my desk for a long time, wondering why I didn't feel his death at the time. But I feel it now, a massive emptiness inside of me that is comforting in its way.

The last article I read before leaving to attend our company's holiday party at a midtown tavern is a longer piece by Advani, in which she lists all the possible victims during Adam Chapman's reign of terror. At the very end of the piece, she mentions both Joanna Davies and Ashley Smith. And then she mentions me. The last line of the article reads: "And then there is Emma Chapman, Adam's twin sister, rumored to have moved to Italy while in her early twenties. Is she another victim, buried somewhere on the grounds of Starvewood Hall? Or is she hiding herself because of what she knows about her twin brother? The police are actively seeking her whereabouts."

CHRISTMASTIME IS HERE AGAIN. AND I AM WAITING, AS I AL-ways do, for one or more guests. I know that Ashley will visit.

Will she understand that I had something to do with what has transpired this year? All I did was throw a pebble into a still pond. The ripples did the rest. I suspect she will know all about it. As she likes to tell me, she knows everything.

What other guests might arrive? I picture a knock on the door, a flashed badge, the return of a disused name. If it happens, it happens. I suppose I am prepared.

I decide to walk to the party. It is the first really cold night of the year, a sharp wind ripping down the avenues. I huddle in my coat and my cheekbones ache. Outside the tavern a stout man in his red Salvation Army apron rings his bell and sings "Good King Wenceslas" in a baritone voice. I dig in my purse for change and he stares right through me into the middle distance, as though I might not even be there. It is, after all, the season of ghosts.

WHY I WROTE
THE CHRISTMAS GUEST

Ever since I was young, I've associated Christmastime with reading. It was partly that I was given books to read for the holidays, and partly that the weather outside was frightful (I grew up in New England), and partly that there was a lot of free time around the Christmas week, but mostly, it was simply because I loved reading, and still do. And while I like Christmas stories, what I really love are Christmas mysteries. They make a lot of sense. Friends and family gathered together in country houses with snow piling up outside. Lots of drinking and resentment. Perfect recipe for a murder.

A couple of years ago I got an idea for a Christmas story of my own. It was about an American college student named Ashley Smith studying for a year in London with no plans to return to her home over Christmas break. She is invited to a friend's house in the Cotswolds for the holidays, a visit that happens in 1989. Tragic events occur during that Christmas week and they reverberate through time when Ashley Smith's diary is reread in modern-day Manhattan.

Often, when I write, I picture my ideal reader. For *The Christmas Guest* I imagined someone on Christmas Eve, the dinner dishes cleaned, one last eggnog in hand, a comfy chair, and a dying fire. Most importantly, I wanted to write a story that could be read in one sitting. *The Christmas Guest* is a short novel, or more accurately, a novella. I've always loved crime and mystery novellas and short novels. The big novel has its place, but there is something particularly special about the short mystery novel, about a story simple enough to be told in about a hundred pages.

There are a lot of Christmas tropes in my story. I didn't want to just write a mystery story that happens to take place at Christmastime. I wanted all the trimmings. Cozy house with Christmas decorations. Roast dinners. Pine boughs. Christmas carols. Snow. But I also wanted it to be dark. Ultimately this is a story about how the yearly arrival of Christmas can be either a blessing or a curse. If something bad happens to someone at Christmas, then how do they avoid the yearly reminders, the onslaught of festive cheer?

I quite like Christmas myself, but I hope this is a book for those who love the holidays as well as for those who'd just as soon give them a pass. And I hope it's a book for everyone who enjoys a little murder dropped into the festivities. Merry Christmas everyone, and an equally exuberant Bah Humbug as well.